# They Always Wave Goodbye

*stories by*

# Katie Sherman

*Finishing Line Press*
Georgetown, Kentucky

# They Always Wave Goodbye

Publisher: Leah Huete de Maines

Editor: Christen Kincaid

Author Photo: Meredith June of Meredith June Photography

Cover Design: Gwen Holt Designs

Order online:  www.finishinglinepress.com
              also available on amazon.com

Author inquiries and mail orders:
Finishing Line Press
P. O. Box 1626
Georgetown, Kentucky 40324
U. S. A.

# Table of Contents

The Fairy House.................................................................. 1

The Easiest Thing............................................................... 9

The Third Gender ............................................................ 12

Hook Wounds................................................................... 26

They Always Wave Goodbye.......................................... 40

Ten Things ........................................................................ 50

Incompetent ..................................................................... 62

The Special One ............................................................... 67

Peanuts And Rubies ........................................................ 69

A Piece Of Me .................................................................. 78

Fear .................................................................................... 88

Short Dogs, Tall Grass..................................................... 90

Love, Mom........................................................................ 100

*For my mom.*

No one understands the sleepless nights, endless worries, or the tiresome toddler conversations until they are parents themselves. In the aftermath of motherhood, I am in awe of your grace. Thank you for having high standards and ensuring I met them. Thank you for putting up with the bratty teenage years and for cultivating a friendship into adulthood.

In short, thank you for being mine.

# The Fairy House

MY Mama was known for flinging lies at strangers. She told people on the Amtrak that she was a country singer. She told one of the church ladies in town that Daddy's an Orthodox Jew. "Why else wouldn't he join us on Sundays?" Mama asked with a casual shrug.

I remember her straightening her spine, sitting ramrod tall, and telling a stranger about a fish she'd once caught. We were at the Five & Dime, this big thrift shop with broken toys and chair frames stripped of upholstery, and globes, more globes than I've ever seen. Red globes and blue ones. Globes lit up from within. Globes you could draw on with chalk. All those globes reminded me of the places I'd never been but wanted to visit. Mama was looking for kitchen stools that could be salvaged, though I still don't know what was wrong with the tall kitchen stools we had. We ran into a friend of hers from high school and they got to talking with the owner about how good a fisherman Mama was.

"She caught more whoppers than you've seen," the man said with a sly wink.

"One was bigger than a truck tire," Mama said. "Scales so shiny it looked like a diamond doused in glitter. He was pretty, but that's nothing compared to how he tasted."

Then she barked her laugh, a hoarse sound that sprung from her like a Jack-in-the-Box with a loose spring, and pulled my sister and me tight against her bony hips. Later, as she tucked us in, Bailey asked, "How big was it really Mama?"

Mama sunk her shoulder into the mattress, nudged her forehead and nose against Bailey's cheek. "As big as my palm." Her lips smacked together noisily as she kissed Bailey hard. "But he did taste good."

The truth in Mama's life was that it was all a lie. She had an unquenchable desire for more. More than her girls or Daddy. More than the two-bedroom house nestled in a deep holler where the soot from coal trucks covered every surface. More than a husband who loved her hard and often but still played pool every night. Sometimes the nagging need for more was a woodpecker on her window that wouldn't go away.

All the wants ate at her, and she called these dips in her personality "the lows." On good days, Mama slunk from her room in a cloud of cigarette smoke with a to-do list a mile long. She made biscuits with sunny side eggs and split sausage patties. Sometimes she'd let us mix three sugary cereals together and eat breakfast in front of the TV. But during the lows, Mama wore a stained yellow nightgown that stretched wide over her breasts and hips. She woke with a migraine, and light and noise and scented candles and sausage patties and everything related to us were triggers. I hid scissors and dishwasher tablets and the kitchen knives, anything that could be perceived as a threat, in the fairy house in our backyard.

The fairy house was a pine cottage Daddy built before they brought me home from the hospital. It smelled like sawdust and new packs of construction paper and finger paint. It was a clubhouse for my *Little House on the Prairie* set and my easel, the best hiding place. As I got older, Mama, Daddy, and I couldn't stand shoulder to shoulder in the fairy house without one of us turning sideways. I had painted the door bright yellow and stacked the window box high with soil and pansies. When Bailey was born, six years after me, no one expected me to introduce her to the fairy house. But when Bailey was three, Mama got the lows. Bailey was pawing at her, and every time Bailey touched her, Mama grimaced, as if her skin was getting singed. I carried Bailey to the fairy house and let her knock over my things. I smeared her hands—wet and sticky with paint—and together, we branded the walls with our handprints. We sat until the firefly wings buzzed around us, and I whispered to her, "This is when the fairies come to paint the sky black." It's what Mama said to me on nights when it was just the two of us. Bailey smiled wide, her peach hand lightly grazing the top of my spine as she patted my back.

In the winter of my senior year, my greatest fear, what I'd been preparing for, happened. Mama tried to commit suicide. Bailey and I found her stretched in a wide X on the black-and-white tile floor of her bathroom.

When Bailey and I were younger, Mama and Daddy would have us pose like misshapen starfish on the hot asphalt in front of our house. The blacktop burnt the chubby undersides of our arms but we giggled as they made chalk outlines. Daddy always had a lukewarm beer and sometimes, while he drew, Mama poured long gulps into the grass and ashed her Marlboro on top. While we colored the shapes, Mama made fried peanut butter and jelly sandwiches. Bailey and I dipped them in milk as she and I ate at the splintered picnic table in front of the fairy house.

So Mama looked like one of those colorless chalk outlines. I knelt to touch her limbs, looking behind my shoulders for Bailey. Mama's arms and legs felt cold. Both wrists were covered in some mixture of dried and wet blood. The razor blade was just out of her grasp. Her tongue hung from her mouth and it looked like she'd eaten a purple lollipop. We'd come home early because Bailey had a croupy cough that rattled her chest and rib cage. Even if we hadn't come early, we still would've found her. A searing anger flooded my sinuses, and hot tears fell swiftly down my cheeks at this realization. A minute later, Bailey walked into the bathroom behind me, nearly tripping over my stalled frame.

"Shit," she gasped, biting hard on her lower lip.

She applied pressure to Mama's wrists with a frayed towel.

"Call 911," she yelled. And again, "Call 911. Hurry."

I brought in the cordless phone, but the hollow voice that spoke didn't sound like mine. I gave our address. I asked them to hustle then bristled as I realized the word was Mama's. Her command as she demanded cooperation. Her plea on mornings when we were hopelessly late. While I lingered on the phone listening to bad elevator music, I looked at Bailey. Her long strawberry blond hair and pale skin, so pale it was basically cellophane, was Mama's. She was prettier than me but I was supposed to be stronger, more in control. The role reversal now was unsettling. Bailey stared at the ceiling and then, looked hard at me.

"I always thought Daddy would go first," Bailey said, her voice low so the operator wouldn't hear.

"Just wander away like a stray cat," I replied through tears and panic, the vocal equivalent of a Jell-O salad.

"It's just us," Bailey said, a bare truth I recognized.

I opened my mouth to say, *What about next year? What about the application I'd mailed for early acceptance to WVU a few months before? What about the rest of the world? The globes?* No sound came out.

We peered at one another, separated by six years and by the thin body of our nearly dead mother and by two pools of blood that seeped into the tile grout. The heat coughed through our house, making my armpits sweat. When the EMTs arrived with their flurry of activity, I stood close to Bailey. Our pink hands were stained with Mama's blood. I squeezed Bailey's hand into my own. Pressure. Release. I'm here. Gone. Adrenaline coursed through me as we stepped into the ambulance and watched them hook Mama to a machine that would fill her with a stranger's blood. I tried not to cry and failed, leaving deep red tracks down my face. Some part of me knew Mama was capable of this. Some part of me wished I were wrong. A foreign voice whispered, *Is this salvation or damnation? A blessing or a curse?*

The drone of the hospital's air conditioner circulated a frigid blast. Both the noise and the cold were imposing. I flattened my palm on Mama's skin. She felt like the day-old snow we used to pack tight when we built snowmen, donning caps of itchy pink wool she had knitted. Mama's legs and stomach and face were bloated from the liquids they'd given her. Daddy arrived just after us, an emergency call summoning him from the bowels of the mine. Bailey and Daddy slumped against one another, shoulder to shoulder on a small gray couch. Bailey had a square stain of blood on one knee. It looked like the state of Wyoming, an ominous square that reminded me of fifth grade when Mama taught me all the state capitols. With a book splayed across her lap, her legs pinched together, she quizzed me. "Cheyenne," I answered and Mama flicked a tongue against the back of her teeth as she spoke. "That's a pretty name," she said with a wink, her blonde eyelashes braided together for a moment. "Smart girl." I basked beneath her subtle praise.

"How did we get here?" I asked, my voice an echo in the cramped hospital room. Neither Bailey nor Daddy answered but the question was a tangible thing, a puzzle piece fitting easily, inevitably into our lives.

Bailey swung her feet, scuffing the blemished floor. Her hands were shoved deep in her pockets, but I could still see her fingers moving, possibly grazing a smooth stone from the creek bed behind our house or a worn and veiny leaf. Mama's room was depressingly bare. No balloons or flowers or teddy bears. There was a phone with a curled tail, wound endlessly around itself. The lights were bright, so bright I squinted to see through them. Mama was unconscious. Not sleeping. Not peaceful. Not dead. Her arm was packed heavy with gauze and tape. Blood was being pumped back into her veins. As it warmed her limbs and brightened her cheeks, it congealed and burped, competing with the sound of the air conditioner.

I couldn't curl myself around her because Bailey and Daddy were watching. I didn't think to build a shield, from either Mama or Bailey. I didn't know whom I most wanted to protect.

Bailey stood, crossed the room in a graceful ballerina glide. She coughed into the crook of her arm.

"We should've known," she said, resting her head on my bicep. She felt warm in contrast to Mama. I shrugged her from me and sat on the floor beside the low hospital bed. I yanked my knees to my chest and rested my head on the bony caps. When I lifted my head a few moments later, Bailey was back on the couch with Daddy. Her eyes were pinched tightly together, her fists accentuated by white rosebud knuckles. *I should hug her,* I thought but couldn't rise to do so. Daddy hiccupped then belched, and an undercurrent of stale Pabst danced lightly around us. I lifted Mama's fingers and snaked them into my thick knot of hair. Hair she had combed and conditioned and braided in a fishtail more times than I could imagine. More times than I would know. I wanted Mama to wake up. To kiss my cheeks. To tell me what a smart girl I was.

The stillness filled the space around us like unwelcome company.

Daddy was useless. He wasn't massaging the moment into submission or normalcy.

I don't know when Bailey inched her way back to me, but I felt her before I saw her. She lifted a small, pale hand to my face. Perhaps to brush the loose wisps of my mane from my forehead the way Mama would, but she stopped midway, thinking better of it. On her elbow, I noticed a small constellation of freckles. Mama had those, too. I opened my mouth to say that, then receded, knowing it could only hurt her more. We sat, crisscross-applesauce on the linoleum, and I slid a little closer. Away from Mama. I laid a hand on her elbow, on the freckled star structure. I covered it, erased it, and together we watched Mama's chest rise and fall beneath the thin white sheet.

Later that night, after we visited Mama, I was the one who cleaned the bathroom. My knees throbbed as I Cloroxed the tiles. I threw the razor in the trash bin. I threw her clothes in, too, brown pants with pleats and a lavender shirt with delicate pearl buttons. And then, when I got rid of the clothes, I bleached the floor again. This time I scrubbed until my hands were raw and my eyes watered from the smell and my nose itched. I scrubbed that floor every day for a week but there was always a thin gray line laced in the grout, just in front of the tub. It seemed like I could see it even after the tiles were replaced two weeks later with gleaming white squares.

The following week, Bailey started her period. I found her in Mama's bathroom with blood swirling through the bowl. She hadn't called Daddy. She'd spent the entire school day in pants marinated in her own blood. The smell was acrylic and too familiar. She leaned her head against the toilet, her hands propped against her stomach. She looked too small to have a period, to be in middle school, to live without her parents. I walked to Magic Mart and bought her a large package of pads, then showed her how to position them in her panties, how to fold the plastic wings over to secure their placement.

"You want to talk about it?" I asked. I was washing the jeans in the bathroom sink with a combination of dish soap and water.

"I'd rather kill myself," Bailey said. Even though it was hyperbolic, I stopped, my hands a little sore as the pink water slunk down the drain. "Sorry," she muttered, looking down. She popped her knuckles. "What did Mama say to you? When you started?"

It was summer and I had a yellow two-piece I wanted to wear to the pool. I knew my period would cut into that. I watched my belly grow wide and swollen. I remembered feeling all the water throughout my body.

"Did she say you were a woman?" Bailey asked. Her voice trembled with optimism.

"I don't think so," I said. I paused, thinking hard about the moment without any real recollection to it. "She showed me what to do. She stocked the freezer with icebox cake and Girl Scout cookies. She took me to the gas station. We got Coke in glass bottles and poured peanuts in it," I lied.

"Mama was good at the little stuff."

Bailey ran her fingers along the smooth pedestal sink. She looked down the drain where so much blood had recently gone. "I'm going to lay down," she said but instead of walking down the hall to our bedroom, she headed straight through the French doors in the back, and ducking her head, slipped into the fairy house. She was out there the entire evening. I made chicken pot pie thick with brown gravy and cubed carrots and finally walked out back and hollered for Bailey.

"Dinner," I yelled. Daddy was still at the pool hall. He'd make a meal of Pabst Blue Ribbon and maraschino cherries. "Bailey," I called again. I walked cautiously out to the fairy house, the frozen grass crunching slightly beneath me.

"I want to see the fireflies," she said as I opened the door. The fairy house smelled like mildew.

"It's too cold, Bails," I said, folding myself onto the plywood. The two of us took up all the space the little house provided. I looked out the square windows that were eye-level, even though we sat. I exhaled. My breath was a visible cloud kneeling at the base of the mountains that hovered against our yard, eavesdropping on our conversation. I shivered against a brisk breeze. "We should go inside."

Bailey was fidgeting, rubbing something in her pocket again. The gesture reminded me of the hospital.

"What's in your pocket?" I asked. She hesitantly yanked out a thin letter on expensive cardstock. The state seal was stamped in the upper left corner, embossed in gold. I ran my fingers over the words *Montani Semper Liberi*. I said it aloud to myself, remembered the phrase from my seventh grade West Virginia History class.

"What's it mean?" Bailey asked.

"Mountaineers are always free," I said, though the walls and the hills suddenly felt a bit claustrophobic to me.

"Are we?" she asked. "I opened it before we found Mama."

Her voice trailed off and I slid the letter from the envelope.

"I was bringing it to you when we found her," she said, an uncharacteristic wavering clashing with her voice.

I read the letter once. Then again.

"I got in," I said, looking at Bailey to uncover what reaction I was allowed to have.

"I know." She smiled and looked out the window, running her fingers against the wooden sill to avert meeting my eyes. "Will you go?"

The question felt aggressive and loaded. I didn't have an answer now, with Mama gone and Daddy gone and Bailey's eyes avoiding mine.

"Will you go with me?" I asked. I needed her and wanted her and yet, I knew the question was a fantasy. A plaything in a play place.

"No," she said simply, her vacant expression fixed on her feet. My heart broke a little. "Let's eat," she said, and I was happy for the distraction. Relieved that no anger penetrated Bailey's voice.

I couldn't sleep that night. It felt like I was drowning within the sheets. The next day, I drove to the mental institute to see Mama, the letter in the back pocket of my jeans. Daddy's maroon Taurus groaned slightly as I took each curve. The institute was a non-descript tan building beside an abandoned Sears. There were no windows on the first three floors. A common room that attendants affectionately referred to as the "game room" was situated in the back. I would have coined it the drool room as all the patients sat in tattered robes with stationary eyes fixated on their flimsy slippers. Its doors opened to a brick patio interspersed with rows of succulents. The garden was surrounded by a tall chain link fence adorned with barbed wire.

Mama didn't rise to greet or hug me. She sat, looking out at the plants.

"Hi, Mama," I said. I leaned down, speaking in a slow, meticulous voice. "You want to walk?"

She nodded and extended her hands for me to pull her up.

We circled the tiny patch of land outside a few times. There were only two wrought iron benches bolted into the bricks, and they were occupied, so we continued to walk in succinct circles. Mama broke the silence.

"In another life, I would be the scuba diver lying at the bottom of a fish tank," she said morosely. "Perfectly encased in water. Buoyant and weightless and unable to talk to anyone."

Her arms were wrapped with gauze that yellowed in the sun. During the two-hour drive, I had folded and refolded the letter until the creases were thin jagged lines against the heavy, fibrous page. I thought of what was under Mama's bandages, the way the cuts formed lopsided V's.

"I never wanted anything as much as I've wanted silence," she said, her face a profile as she pressed her hands against a cactus. "Ouch," she said softly before doing it again.

It felt wrong to talk after that, like something a toddler would do to test her parents. Mama's breath was heavy and ragged, the breath of a jogger rather than a slim, middle-aged mother. Occasionally the breeze would grind against the flimsy metal fence, a needle stabbed into the noiselessness. The only laughter we heard was manic. I thought of Mama's laugh. I thought of the times when I thought she was better, self-corrected. The times when she was wise. I ran my hand against the outline of the square letter still in the back pocket of my jeans. In the end, I stayed for half an hour and drove home. I didn't tell her, unable to see through the fog the institute produced to rescue Mama.

When I got home, I found Bailey in the fairy house. She had uncovered an old Lego set and was constructing a multi-colored tower that brushed the ceiling. She didn't greet me, instead handing me the bag with the blocks. I started adding a layer to the base.

"You have to go," she said, her voice rattling off the walls a little and catching me off guard.

I scraped my index finger against the cuticle of my thumb until a few thin spots of blood emerged.

"It's just us," I said, and Bailey flinched as if her own words were attacking her. She sat next to me.

"What did Mama say?" she asked, though I hadn't told her where I'd been.

"Nothing," I said. I couldn't discuss the drive or the scuba diver or the fenced-in garden with no flowers. I wanted so badly to leave, to go to school, to escape. I wanted so badly to stay.

"It'll always just be us," she said.

We continued to build the tower in silence until the floor was covered in blocks and we no longer fit. Then, Bailey placed her hand in mine. We walked away from the fairy house with its low windows and its piney aroma and the fragments of our childhood.

# The Easiest Thing

LILY'S day starts at 5 a.m. Tiny fingers etch her face—shoving into nostrils, her mouth, her ear canals. Finally, they poke at her eye sockets. Pry the lids as if they are cartoon roller shades. It's not always the same child. Sometimes, it's the boy—his mouth dangling open, inches from her face, breath pungently odorous. Other times, it's the little girl, hair tangled and knotted. Stringy tendrils that tickle her mother's chin. These children press their palms against Lily's sagging breasts, her deflated and scarred stomach. If given the option, she imagines they'd crawl back up, seeking shelter in her womb.

It's as if they made the decision to tag-team torture her. They are never satisfied at the same time. Someone's always crying, taunting, provoking. One or the other continually contributes to the discontent of the household.

Lily fries eggs for breakfast and they dangle from her limbs. They cluster close as soap smatters her wrists while she does the dinner dishes. She can't open a bag of Fritos without them begging like stray mutts, desperate for a bite. When she showers, they open the curtain releasing the steam. Her lap is their seat, their trampoline, at times their toilet.

She prayed for their birth once, willed them into her womb. Scrutinized blurred ultrasounds and tried to count tiny toes. Now, what she prays for is silence. Space. A moment to remember who she used to be. She wants her art. Her creativity. Her babies replaced her essence with something pedestrian.

She is a mother—only a mother.

And so, on a random Friday, her mind is occupied with lists. The grocery list: organic eggs, skim milk, whole wheat bread, Fritos, chicken thighs, Brussels sprouts, taco seasoning. The goods for her alone. Virginia Slims, Bud Light, Oreos. The to do list: laundry, store, carpool, ballet, soccer, bills, dinner, bath time, reading, bedtime. Lily's time? A list of the things she wants: silence, her rough hands manipulating clay, the crisp pages of *Water for Elephants,* her toes curled into the pliable sand of a remote beach. A list of the things she needs: her feather mattress and the pillow she folds in two, her toes painted Nars' Soup Can Red, the droning scream of bad reality television.

Lily's eyes rest on the art supplies splayed across the living room. Stickers, markers, and construction paper. Glue and Play-Doh. Watercolors and brushes. Lily cleaned the room earlier, scrubbed and swept the night before when everyone else snored absentmindedly. She removed miniature fingerprints from glass surfaces. She prayed as she cleaned, asking or begging for a return to her sanity.

Now, Lily is drowning within the mess. She turns in a slow circle, surveying the damage.

She knows she can leave. She could flee from the lists and the obligations. The invisible husband and the faceless kids she created. The one that has her eyes. The daughter with her curls. She could get a hotel room in a seedy beach town where no one would look for her. She could have a life of isolation. She could be whoever she wanted.

Lily begins collecting the slender paintbrushes. She picks the clotted Play-Doh from the wool carpet while fantasizing about her escape. In her head, she scribbles a note. I can't … it reads. She doesn't think it needs further explanation, but she could elaborate.

*I can't wake up to another morning of endless invasion.*

*I can't care about one more argument.*

Lily accidentally kicks over a small plastic cup of cloudy water hidden within the mess. Rather than scrambling for a towel to absorb it, she watches it seep into an oblong stain that closely resembles a thought bubble with no thought inside.

*I can't threaten one more timeout.*

*I can't be the only one who cares about our house. My time. Our kids.*

Construction paper is stacked on every surface. Some of the brightly colored pages have one swirl. Lily stares at the waste, considers throwing it all away. Not just the art supplies but the toys and the ragged stuffed animals her kids love. She sifts casually through her daughter's drawings, not knowing what she's looking for and yet, looking for something all the same. In the center of the pile, there's a drawing done with permanent markers. Lily lifts it closer to her face and allows the smell to assault her. The name at the bottom of the page catches her attention. It's written in a slanted diagonal. The "E" has one too many lines. The dot over the "I" is bigger than the letters. The stick on the "A" is on the wrong side. Something about the childish script is endearing though. The handwriting looks a little like Lily's.

The picture is more detailed than the others. It's clearly a person, a woman with long brown hair and an asymmetrical smile. The gold triangle on her head could be a beehive but Lily knows it's a crown. At first she thinks Elaine has drawn a princess and she rolls her eyes at the triteness. Then, she takes in the swirl of gold inside a sunflower hand. Lily traces the blue and red dress. Just above the round hand is a square splash of yellow. A cuff.

Lily smiles, thinking of the trip to the comic book store. The rickety place smelled like wet newspapers and moth balls. The walls were covered with shelves that held figurines of Superman, Spiderman, Batman. Thor's hammer hung adjacent to a lit light saber. Elaine had spent the evening before discussing the merits of Elsa versus Ariel versus Cinderella until it became too much. Lily looked the comic book store up online, her fingers bashing the keys with some mixture of anger and annoyance over her daughter's stereotypical cartoon choice. She bought twenty comics and two figurines. Lily had lectured Elaine about the need to save yourself. To be your own superhero. She thought it had fallen on deaf ears. She imagined the Wonder Woman money was wasted. But Elaine had drawn her. Lily alone can decipher the image. Only she knows her child well enough to glance into her imagination. Lily mentally crumples her escape note.

She could walk away and be the missing link from their childhood. *The easiest thing.*

Or she could stay. She could raise them and fuck them up and help them and hinder them. She could teach them her values. She could influence them even if she didn't realize it in the moment. She hugs Elaine's picture to her chest.

Lily surveys the mess. She could hate them even as she loves them harder.

Wouldn't that be the easiest thing?

# The Third Gender

THE plane skipped through the pockets of turbulence like pebbles on a pond. Thin, gray vinyl seats made Nadia's skin itch. Her legs were encased in flesh-colored compression socks that sometimes made her pulse quicken. Nadia's brown hair was tied in a messy bun, tendrils falling down the nape of her neck. The camera sat in her lap; its black buttons beckoned her. When she traveled, Nadia's first picture was always from the plane. In the states, she looked for the symmetrical angles of Little League fields—white plates, red clay, pure green grass. In London, she focused on the bridges—fishbone scales of ecru against the murky water. In Egypt, Nadia noticed the buildings—tall skyscrapers that seemed to rise from the sand itself. She scratched her left hand, focused the lens, and slowly applied pressure to the shutter. Moments later, the plane bounced three quick times and rolled to a stop.

Nadia had been arguing over her place as a war correspondent since she graduated from Medill nine years ago. There was still something taboo about women in combat zones. But now that she was five months pregnant, the stares and warnings were so redundant she regularly ignored them. Her mother sent pleading emails of concern, guilting her. Jonathan, the baby's father, wanted her to exclusively take local assignments. After he suggested this one too many times, their relationship unspooled like yarn dropped to the floor. Post bitter break-up and determined to make a feminist statement, Nadia finagled a job with The Associated Press as a stringer. She was penetrating the Libyan insurgence, risking her life and that of her unborn son for a nominal wage. During previous assignments, she had seen car bombs and grenades, chemical weapons and famine. She saw babies with bloated, distended bellies and visible rib cages. She'd heard cries so raw they were terrestrial as they imprinted themselves permanently in her mind. She'd been shot at. She'd been injured. But none of that could keep Nadia from the field. Work was an escape. Her job placed her in situations where she witnessed first-hand the cruelty and benevolence of humanity. Nadia had a partiality for Arabic countries, a preference passed down from a mentor who revealed that female journalists had an advantage there.

"In a lot of places, but mostly Islamic societies, we're the third gender," this mentor had said over cocktails in a crowded, low-rent bar when they were imbedded in Afghanistan. "Unlike men, we can speak to Islamic women, but the men view us as more male than female. It's the one advantage we get."

They'd toasted one another then, their lukewarm beer skunked and reeking of yeast.

This trip, Nadia traveled light with two small leather bags worn around the edges and consistently dusted with sand. Her heaviest was her camera case, a graduation present from her parents that had seen nearly forty countries. It held her two favorite DSLR bodies, three lenses, an independent strobe flash, a modifier, ten flash cards, a stack of erotic letters that helped with checkpoints, Leo's sonogram, and a smudged and wrinkled photocopied picture of Martha Gellhorn. Part of her felt guilty that she stared at the image of her idol more than the ultrasound of the fuzzy jellybean that would be her son.

Nadia stepped directly from the airport's entrance to the asphalt surrounding it, searching for her escort. The weather was balmy and tropical with humidity that hung around Nadia's shoulders. She knew only two things. Her escort would be a man and he would be young. Guides were almost always English-speaking students. Muhammad stood beside a beat-up black SUV. In a sea of hijabs and aging men, he wore a New York Yankees hat with a black insignia and camo background. It was pulled low over deep-set brown eyes. He was the type of man who shouldn't have a beard but he did. His was filled with a handful of bald patches. The peninsulas of hair were black and wiry. He wore a blue shirt buttoned to his neck, and it looked like his Adam's apple was erupting over it. He stepped forward, extending his hands to accept the bags. A musk that was pleasant but overwhelming rose from him.

"Here," he said eagerly. "I'll get that."

Nadia readjusted the camera bag on her shoulder, allowing the weight to cut into the pale skin beneath her tunic. She handed Muhammad the smaller duffle that carried her maternity pants, body armor, pajamas, and a few packs of Nutter Butters to ward off nausea. Muhammad fumbled with the single bag and aggressively opened the rear door. Nadia clambered into the front instead.

Muhammad kicked the tires and clumps of red clay poured down. "Most journalists ride in the rear," he said.

Nadia pulled at the edge of a red Nutter Butter packet, biting into the cookie and allowing the creamy peanut butter to coat her tongue. "I'd prefer the company." She held out the bag. "Want one?" Muhammad snaked a hand through the opening in the cellophane, took one, and began to chew loudly. The air conditioning blasted air as Nadia wiggled in the seat to get comfortable. Muhammad walked around the tail of the vehicle before flopping into the driver's seat. He adjusted the angles of the vents and navigated the car onto a narrow side street adjacent to the airport.

"You're from Egypt?" Nadia asked Muhammad as he shifted gears, careful to ensure their forearms didn't graze.

"Ajdabiya," he said. He stared directly ahead as he steered the car onto a two-lane road surrounded by a residential neighborhood.

"Your family's there?" Nadia asked, referring to the coastal town in Libya now infamous for protecting a mob that attacked four European journalists. Muhammad nodded. The wind rattled the windshield as they drove through a neighborhood with tall stucco apartment buildings, laundry hanging on stretched lines across the roof.

"Most of them are still there. There were eleven of us," he said. "Eight girls, me, my parents."

"Are you close?" Nadia chewed slowly, careful to ensure she wasn't loud. Jonathan once claimed her chewing sounded like grinding bolts.

"I was close to my oldest sister," he said, allowing the word was to dominate.

"And now?"

"She was a refugee in Tunisia," he said, the words coming slowly. "There was a garbage fire in the camp. She tried to help a few children who were watching the flames. She couldn't."

Nadia closed her eyes. She instinctively rubbed her stomach, and her son savagely kicked her hand. She stared out the window. During the next three hours, most of the villages that skirted Nadia's peripheral vision looked similar: grungy white walls and arched windows coated with iron bars. In the seaside village of Marsa Matruh, black graffiti covered the houses' lower halves but it wasn't the foul language of New York vandals. There were a number of mocking portraits of Gaddafi, meticulously drawn, with oversized ears and wide, cartoonish eyes. Nadia snapped a quick picture of one.

"Why are you here?" Muhammad asked after they passed Marina El Alamein and had been on the road thirteen hours. He flexed his fist. Nadia watched the veins bulge. She hadn't expected the question. Even more puzzling was his tone, a tone that was neither aggressive nor friendly. It teetered somewhere arbitrarily in between.

"I don't know. Maybe I have something to prove." Nadia gnawed on the outer edge of her tongue. The raised taste buds were metallic, like pennies. "Are you angry I am?"

"You'll have a family soon. Why put yourself in the middle of this chaos?"

"It's my job," Nadia answered, annoyed, but also aware that it wasn't the whole truth. Her answer was far too simple. She paused but no dramatic effect was created. "My dad calls me Shark because sharks never stop moving. They're in perpetual motion. I just, I don't know who I am without a camera."

"What happens when the baby comes?" The question surprised her, and the intrusion felt like a nagging needle in her spine. She tried her best to ignore it, knowing she was guilty of peppering Muhammad with questions as well.

Nadia rested her head against the cool glass and allowed awkwardness to fill the car. They bounced over a rut, and Nadia's camera slipped from her lap. She needed a moment to erase the question, so she retrieved the camera, raised it to her right eye, and took an errant picture of the coast. The camera felt heavy in her hands. Leaden. Waves peaked and broke in a foamy froth. *What happens when the baby comes?* Nadia pictured Jonathan's murky gray eyes. The way he squinted when he read in their dimly-lit living room, his fingers prying at the frayed edge of the sofa. When Nadia imagined her son, he was a carbon copy of his father.

\*\*\*

In the border town of Salloum, Muhammad stopped at an open-air fish market that smelled of dust and salt and the blood from mackerels. The fish were packed tightly, balancing on back fins. Their eyes were unnerving—staring up at Nadia as she passed. The scarf tied tightly under her chin absorbed her sweat. She tucked it behind her ears before readjusting it so her hair wouldn't show. Broad men in green aprons stood and sliced thin slivers of the fish's fleshy underbelly. They would extend bloody knives to the people, offering a taste of fresh sashimi. Nadia snapped a photo, but only one, to relieve some of her discomfort.

Muhammad ducked into a restaurant and Nadia followed a few paces behind. Wooden stools sat underneath rickety tables with iron legs. They ordered a fish skillet. Two gray plates were slathered with yellow rice, peas, and oversized prawns the size of a millionaire's engagement ring. Momentarily forgetting where she was, Nadia slipped off her shoes. Her compression socks had left deep red indentions on her ankles and heels. She began to peel them off.

"Confining?" Muhammad asked, blushing slightly presumably at the sight of a woman's bare ankle. Nadia nodded, rubbed the indention, and put the socks back on.

Muhammad crushed a lemon in his fist over the food. He ate quickly.

"How are we going to get through the border?" she asked. She was becoming unnerved by the lack of a plan. A thin bead of sweat formed at the base of Nadia's neck. During the drive, she hadn't slept much and Muhammad hadn't slept at all. It was too intimate, the thought of closing her eyes, drooling, snoring, sighing next to this man she barely knew. Muhammad preferred to drive straight through. When he stopped for gas, Nadia stretched and walked. Muhammad ordered tea in oversized paper containers. The heat turned his palms a deeper shade of red.

"Anything?" she asked again.

Muhammad continued to chew loudly.

"I have these letters," she began, knowing that Muhammad wouldn't like them. This was Jonathan's idea, something he'd heard other female journalists used. A stack of erotic letters strategically aged with tea, to distract young guards. Often the boys stood drooling with quickened pulses over references to pink clitorises and rosy nipples. *The color of femininity was a blush, blooming pink*, Nadia thought, knowing she owned nothing that color.

"They're sexual," she said. "Distracting."

Muhammad worked hard to continue eating, but blood filled his neck and jawline. The exposed skin throughout his beard was pink.

"Unsavory," he mumbled. "Disgraceful."

"They work. The letters will get us through."

"No. You don't have credentials?" His mouth was still filled with food.

"I'm here to report on the rebels," she said and wondered how much Muhammad knew about her assignment. Did he support Gaddafi? "If you have no plan, the letters will have to do."

"What do they say in your country?" Muhammad asked. "It's your rodeo." There was a catch in his voice. A pucker that made Nadia think he was aiming for nonchalance. "We obviously can't take weapons in, but you'll wear your body armor."

Nadia balked at the suggestion, a vein in her neck throbbing like a recently stubbed toe. Jonathan would have asked her to take such a precaution. He would have massaged the muscles in her shoulder blades as he told her how necessary it was. Goosepimples spread like a rash over Nadia's forearms. She didn't want to miss him.

At the car, Muhammad crumpled trash in his fist, tightly squeezing the Nutter Butter packages like a stress ball. He tossed the overnight bag onto the gravel parking lot.

"The armor will protect you," he said.

"It might keep me from getting across the border." An Iraqi Army sergeant once told her body armor was a red flag in unstable political climates. It meant she needed protection by both inanimate objects and his people. The sergeant hovered near her, so close she could smell the Skoal on his breath. So close she could hear his jaw click as he spat.

"Not if your letters are all you say they are," Muhammad said, bringing her back. He kicked at the clumps of dirt and small rocks.

Nadia pulled the gauzy charcoal tunic over her head. Underneath, she wore a stretchy flesh-colored tank top and jeans. Muhammad stared intently at his palms, wiping them on his khakis.

"There's a restroom inside," he said gruffly. "Doing that here is just foolish." His jaw was a tense line. "Remember where you are."

Nadia climbed into the car, slamming the door behind her. She positioned the mesh harness across her chest, pulling the shoulders straps taut and securing the Velcro. The bulky vest constricted her back and torso, causing Nadia to instantly sweat and pant. The vest would've come just under her belly had she not been pregnant. But now, it was even with her stomach. An armor belly shirt. She stretched the sheaths as far as they would go and lightly folded them over. Barely an inch or two to spare. Her headscarf sat six inches from her forehead. Thin wisps of hair were plastered to the corner of her eyes. Glued to her cheeks. Nadia's eyes watered, and she wondered if they were tears from the disagreement or the sudden homesickness or the embarrassment of her rookie mistake. She stepped from the car, her tunic in place. Nadia shifted, rolling her belly back and forth as she tested her agility within the armor.

"I'll humor you now," she said. "But in the field, I can't get around with both the baby's weight and the weight of the vest."

Muhammad rolled his eyes, still staring off into the distance. He crossed his arms begrudgingly as Nadia spoke, then walked to the other side of the car.

The border was crowded with long lines of cars. Many were piled high with rolled rugs and filled laundry bags. The air smelled like sand and sweat, like a feral animal. As Muhammad steered through the traffic, Nadia snapped a picture of three little girls. There was dew in their hair, evidence of the cool nights.

If it weren't for the odd background—the piles of clothes and the mass of people—the scene would feel pedestrian. A man leaned arrogantly in front of a wall of garbage bags selling bottles of water, flashlights, batteries. His long black beard was freckled with white hairs. Muhammad spoke to him, and he began flailing his arms wildly.

"Who was that?" Nadia asked after they drove away. Muhammad accelerated too quickly and a fume of smoke engulfed the man.

"Kadar. A friend I see when I cross," Muhammad said. "There's a guy in the far lane. Kadar says that guy will let us through, papers or not, when given the hand signal."

Nadia rummaged through her camera case for the erotic letters but they weren't there. There were ten total but the one on the bottom was the only letter that was real. It was pristinely white and crisp. It was from Jonathan, and unlike the others, the letter outlined life rather than sex. Nadia had always loved his slanted script as he spelled out things like procreation and legacy and son. The words beat against her like pellets in a hailstorm. It had been Jonathan's idea to get pregnant. His idea to carry the letters. His idea to end things. It was Jonathan who wanted the child she carried. She had the proof. She had it all in writing. The letters weren't where she'd placed them. She shifted through the bag again, more frantically this time. Removed camera bodies. The sonogram. Gellhorn.

"They're not there," Muhammad said as he pressed one finger on the barely visible creases in his forehead. "I took them. At the market."

"Give them back," Nadia said, her voice sliding an octave higher.

"That filth," Muhammad said. He looked like he wanted to wipe his tongue clean. "That has no place here."

Nadia sat, chastised and angry with the heavy vest constricting her rib cage.

"You could've told me you knew someone." She felt like a child.

Muhammad laughed but the chuckle felt aggressive and taunting. "I didn't know Kadar would be here. That he knew a way through," he said. "I just knew I couldn't use sex to help you pass."

Nadia's eyes bulged and pulsed, vibrating to avoid inevitable tears. That letter was the only proof she'd had that Jonathan wanted them. Now there was nothing.

Muhammad waited at the border. When they finally inched towards the front, Kadar was a few steps behind their car. People flanked him on all sides but he didn't blend. He was heads taller than the tallest man. He stretched a small Libyan flag over his head and Muhammad paused to chat with the guard, passed him a few scraps of paper: a ploy to make it seem like they had documentation. Their accomplice leaned heavily on his forearms and leered at Nadia. She felt clammy, unnerved. Her palms began to sweat. Then he allowed them through. Muhammad stomped on the gas pedal, sailing past the checkpoint as red dust kicked up behind them, and the girls and the tightly rolled red rugs, even Kadar, were visions from the past.

Nadia closed her eyes, unwilling to sleep next to Muhammad but needing distance the car couldn't provide. She knew he'd taken something from her that she shouldn't want, and the betrayal was a burn she couldn't fixate on.

The hotel room in Benghazi was dirty with flittering flecks of dust and smudged glass. There were cockroaches whose exterior shells made loud crunching sounds, even under bare feet. Despite the ugliness and the dirt coating the pastel duvet, the lights in the room were bright fluorescents; bulbs hung so low Nadia bumped her head. The bathtub was marked with a tan ring. The sink was so chipped it looked like cheap confetti, robbed of color.

Nadia opened the closet doors, which groaned. Each of her tunics rested in a single file line, revealing a sampling of dark hues—faded black, putrid green, charcoal. Propped in the corner, heavy and intrusive, was the navy body armor. It was the only pure and saturated color in the room. The Velcro straps hung open, an exposed hug. Nadia kicked it as she dressed. It rocked, teetered one way then another. It rested, still standing and unharmed. Nadia brushed her teeth and dressed quickly. She let the body armor remain in the corner as she pulled the green tunic over her head and hid her hair with a black scarf.

In the lobby, a group of people talked about recent arrests, including a handful of American journalists. Muhammad sat, drank tea, and listened.

"We need to head to Shajara Square," Nadia said, without so much as a greeting. She fiddled with the cumbersome tunic, crumpled and contorted the fabric.

"Too dangerous."

"The revolution is nonviolent, Muhammad," Nadia said, trying not to scoff. "I have to move freely."

"Nonviolence doesn't mean no violence. The people seem nice but there have been grumblings." His voice was irritatingly calm. "Stop being naïve. Something bad could happen to you."

"If I want or need your advice, I'll ask for it," she said. "Get the car."

Muhammad sat his tea down disagreeably, slamming it onto the side table so hard that brown liquid sloshed over the rim. He jiggled the keys in his pocket and walked briskly to the rotating glass door.

The sound from Shajara Square hit Nadia first. Crowds chanted in a low cadence. The eeriness of their rhythm made Nadia shiver despite the heat. Then she saw the horde of protesters. She had been in Benghazi once before and remembered the square housed a wide round fountain, but now it was no longer visible. Instead, black hair and headscarves were sandwiched against one another, charging forward like a storm cloud. Around the fountain was a small city of white tents marred with dust. People held colorful signs, florescent poster board fastened to tree limbs. One had a black and white photo of Gaddafi.

The paper was slashed where his throat would be. Others held Libyan flags, waving them aggressively against the battering wind. The car couldn't navigate the street so they left it parked and scurried into the crowd. Strangers began to crawl on top of the vehicle as soon as Muhammad and Nadia got out, and the hood popped slightly under their weight. Someone bumped into Nadia, pushed her back into a sea of caramel-colored hands. She and Muhammad exchanged a look, their eyes drawn together and their mouths thin, mirrored lines.

"What're they saying?" Nadia asked.

"Corruption is the enemy of God."

The wind picked up and billowed her tunic, then switched directions so the fabric defined her bump. Her camera sat heavy over her stomach. The long lens pinged off people as she worked her way through the crowd. Most protesters were young. One woman had shiny black hair that peeked out from her hijab. A tiny boy wore brown pants that were too small, thick and inappropriate for the weather. Nadia wanted to carry him from this tumultuous place. Another little girl had almond-shaped eyes that were soulful. Her sighs bubbled out, showing how little she wanted to be there. They didn't speak to Nadia, too caught up in the aggression around them, but they stared.

Muhammad shifted cautiously, his eyes busy as he surveyed the crowd. "I don't feel good about this."

The crowd grew louder. Guards waited in the windows of the tall brick government buildings that outlined the square. Nadia's muscles felt like jelly as she raised the camera to her right eye. She took thirty pictures before the first gunshot echoed against the crowd. Muhammad tugged on her elbow, guiding her closer to the city's center. A signal to move on. She didn't stop though. Her pointer finger didn't leave the shutter as she pivoted, getting each angle. Then the woman next to her lit a homemade bomb. She got a picture of the woman— her arm a slingshot, her hijab peeled back to reveal a toned bicep. Her hazel eyes flickering as they gazed beyond the flame. The woman's son clung to the hem of her black hijab. He was probably nine. The flame seared Nadia's eyes. Smoke overwhelmed her, surrounded her like a cloak. The smell jabbed at her, making her retch. Then a ricocheting bullet sliced through the boy's shin. He clutched the wound, folding in half as he fell to the ground. The mother sheltered him with her body, desperation radiating from her. Muhammad squeezed Nadia's forearm as he bent to check on the injured child. Nadia tasted blood. She had bitten her lip so hard, she'd broken the skin.

"We need to leave before things get worse," Muhammad hollered into the violent wind. His fingers left angry red indentions on Nadia's arm. Another bullet buried itself into a myrtle tree, somehow missing every protester despite the confined space.

"This is the story," Nadia yelled. She took pictures from every angle. The signs. The children. The enraged faces. The machine guns. She raised her camera high and captured an image of the crowd. "Closer," and she pulled Muhammad by his sleeve, pointing towards the fountain. He held his hands up, as if in defeat. She led him through the square.

Nadia climbed onto the fountain's beveled edge and pivoted to see where they had been. She snapped a picture of the men scaling their car. They looked about Muhammad's age. Each with beards. One had a vein that pulsed in his forehead. She zoomed in on his face, focused, captured the image. The army released tear gas. It scorched her eyes and burned the inside of her nostrils. She ducked to avoid it. The next bullet lodged itself in Nadia's shoulder blade before she heard it, as if some natural law had worked in reverse, its force pushing her into the fountain. The warm water was dirty, more gray than clear. It smelled like used gym socks, likely a wash station for the protesters who'd camped there overnight. Nadia rubbed it into her eyes anyway, tried to grind away the heat of the mace. Blood ran in a quick, thin line to her waist and she felt for a hole in the front of her body, but there was no exit wound. Her body had accepted the bullet, protected it with surrounding muscles. Nadia felt lightheaded, her entire arm was numb and her fingers tingling.

She rubbed her stomach and wished the baby would move. He didn't. The crowd and the gas and the blood swallowed her. Soon though, a hand gripped the back of her tunic. Muhammad jerked her away from the water, shouting her name. He cradled his right hand and Nadia saw the perfectly round hole. Blood encrusted his wrist.

"We have to get out of here." He supported Nadia as she crawled from the fountain. Nadia shivered. Her clothes clung to her body. Her face felt cold and sore, as if she'd been badly beaten. Her eyes wide, scanning. Her camera was slung behind her, like some useless cape. The leather strap that secured it around her neck was damp but it was otherwise unharmed. Muhammad persistently mumbled, "One, two. One, two." Nadia joined the cadence, counting her steps to keep herself moving. They couldn't focus on a true conversation, on anything more substantial.

"One, two. One, two. One, two," they counted together.

Muhammad and Nadia limped to a doorway at the edge of the square. Nadia slumped against the door, nodded in and out of restless consciousness. Muhammad lightly slapped her cheeks.

"Stay awake, Nadia," he said. Nadia groaned. He shouted her name.

"Tell me about the baby. Tell me what you're going to name your baby."

"Leo," she said, but she knew her voice sounded garbled.

"What does it mean? Here names have meaning."

"It's my dad's name. It means bravery. Brave people."

Muhammad tore Nadia's tunic. He created a few strips from the fabric and tied them around his hand. Then he started to wrap Nadia's shoulder.

"Stubborn," he said again and again, firmly. "Can't wear the armor. Can't leave. Can't take care of yourself."

"Stop," Nadia said. She wanted to stand, to walk away but couldn't find the strength. Muhammad rested her against the doorframe.

"We need to get out of here. Can you walk?" He scratched his beard, dug at the flesh underneath. Then he pulled Nadia to her feet. He propped her against him. "Walk." He slapped her again. "You're in shock but you need to walk." Nadia shuffled her feet slowly. Muhammad lifted her a few inches from the ground, as if they were part of a dangerous three-legged race. They walked that way for ten blocks. Nadia lost consciousness as they climbed into the back of an ambulance.

At Al Hawari, a hospital in the city's center, rows of people were placed on thin blue cots. Women were separated from men. The medics removed Nadia's makeshift bandages and repacked the wounds in an attempt to save blood. Nadia gouged the fleshy heel of her hand with her fingernails as she wriggled with pain. She wore a bracelet, a sterling silver cuff that rattled up and down her arm. Inscribed on it was her blood type, AB Positive, and her allergies, blueberries and strawberries, in a thin, neat print. A Valentine's Day present from Jonathan. A romantic gesture for the travel-savvy. Nadia pressed hard on her stomach. She wanted to feel Leo bump against her. Someone strapped a small ultrasound machine around her belly, and she saw his tiny erratic heartbeat. 156. 162. 158. With each beep, Nadia relaxed a little more.

"She needs blood, and the bullet should be removed," Nadia heard the medics say to a short nurse who looked like a fresh-faced teenager. Nadia's breath quickened and someone placed a plastic oxygen mask over her face.

"The wound is shallow," the girl said. "Numb her."

A bee sting. Her muscles loosened. Her body turned cold. Then, a scraping tug against her shoulder. The girl used the needle to pry the football-shaped bullet from her muscle. When it was released, it pinged into a tin circular dish.

"Gauze and blood," the nurse shouted.

The nurse lightly pushed Nadia up, supporting her with her forearm as she rolled her over and wrapped the cotton in loops around her shoulder. Someone rubbed yellow iodine against the crook of her elbow and hung a bag of blood next to her. It gulped and gargled as it entered her veins. The needle itched as the clotted platelets went through her. Nadia wanted to doze but Leo moved. A happy and safe flip-flop.

***

When Nadia woke, the needle was still buried into a fold of skin. Her arms were yellow from the iodine and red from the blood. She was in a double room. Muhammad lay in a bed next to her, his hand bandaged, his wrist in a white cast. He was also connected to a bag of blood but he was using his free hand to pump it out. The blood was his own. He was donating.

"Hey," she said, and her throat throbbed slightly from the effort. Her voice was hoarse from screaming and the drugs. Muhammad sat up straighter. He continued squeezing a small blue ball in his left hand.

"I asked them to put me in here. I hope you don't mind." He looked down at his paper gown and blushed. Nadia tried to sit up. "Your hand," she said.

"It's okay. My wrist is fractured. The bullet went in and out. Clear exit."

"I lost you out there for a minute." Nadia arched her back. She tried to stretch the sore muscles. The blood going in felt clumpy and intrusive.

"I saw you in that water. Face down but your camera was high over your head. Protecting it."

"Work first," Nadia said, hating the truth in the words.
Muhammad smiled. "I'm sure your other arm cradled Leo."

She didn't recognize herself in that moment or in this one. She felt split, wanting to be a good mother and a journalist. Longing to know how to prioritize both.

"I'm sorry I didn't listen to you."

Muhammad sighed. "You remind me of my sister. The one I told you about before. Aya." Nadia tried to sit up in the bed, to rearrange and give him her undivided attention. Her shoulder and the blood transfusion prevented it, so she stared at the square-paneled ceiling. Muhammad continued: "She was determined to save everything. She taught me English."

"How old were you?"

"Eight." He paused. "She found this book in a second-hand bookstore near our house. *Charlie and the Chocolate Factory.*" Nadia grinned. "She read it to me. She was going to America. She had spoken to a family there about babysitting. She was going to send money and help my sisters get visas."

"What about you?" Nadia asked. She imagined him sitting under the shade of a wide tree reading this book from her childhood. The cookies were different and the scenery was more quaint than the suburb where she was raised but the words were the same. So was the feeling.

"Not too many men get to leave. We're needed for the labor force. Plus, women's lives here are so much worse than mine."

"So you just learned …"

"She got this look when she read. Her eyes would narrow and three tiny wrinkles separated her eyebrows. You get them too. When you look at a picture on your camera."

Nadia closed her eyes, a satisfied smirk staining her face.

"Now what?" Muhammad asked. "Where will you go?"

Nadia lightly scratched the needle incision. "Home. At least for a little while."

She turned her head and watched as a dust storm shook the glass. Fat clumps of red sand spiraled through the air. Because of the wind, everything here tasted slightly of the earth. At first, Nadia thought just the vegetation at the local market tasted like dirt, bright fruit and beans and grains pulled from the ground. But then she realized she smelled dust everywhere. She smelled the dirt in the hospital and in the city square and in the hotel. The musk that rose from Muhammad's skin was mixed with the dust. *Ashes to ashes. Dust to dust*, Nadia recited in her head. Then she reminded herself that she was not dead. Muhammad was not dead. Leo was not dead. She took a long breath and counted to ten.

"Will you come back?"

"I think so. I just need to stand still for a moment."

Nadia pressed the place where her camera normally rested. She held her hand just over Leo.

"I have to do something. Let me call the nurse," she said.

Nadia left her hand on her belly. She felt Leo swim. His movements were like tiny bubbles popping against her stomach lining.

Nadia listened to Muhammad wrestle uncomfortably in the bed. She shoved her hair behind her ears.

The nurse walked in. "What do you need?" she asked. Nadia pointed to the brown case. Muhammad's eyes grew wide, his hands flexing more steadily and quickly now so that the blood belched as it flowed into the bag. He didn't have time to protest.

With her free hand, Nadia pulled the camera from the bag and quickly centered Muhammad in the frame.

# Hook Wounds

MONA cradled the head of a stuffed elephant. She sniffed it, inhaled her daughter Libby's intoxicating scent, a mix of condensed milk and orange Mentos, like the Creamsicles Mona ate as a child. Mona ran her fingers along the edge of the antique changing table, the dresser, the mirror. She didn't touch the crib. She struggled to look at the cushy purple bumper tied to it. The white accent pillow with Libby's initials—LRS—embroidered in lilac was too pristinely white for a nursery. It shouldn't stay so crisp. It should have spit up marks and drool. Signs of life, not death.

*S.I.D.S. Sudden infant death syndrome.* Mona rolled the initials around in her head. *SIDS. LRS. SIDS. LRS.*

"I want this out of my face," she said, more as a distraction to herself than to her husband, Alex who watched from the doorframe.

The movers were coming in an hour, and this was the only room left untouched. Where would the fluffy bunny and the pink piggy bank go? The gauzy white dresses, the size two Pampers, the miniature shoes for feet that couldn't yet walk? Mona couldn't put Libby in a box.

Alex adjusted his glasses, ran a hand through his grey-flecked hair, and stepped into a beam of sunshine. He methodically started to pry the crib bars from their sockets.

"Stop it," Mona said, snarling the words, like gravel under a speeding tire.

Alex furrowed his eyebrows. Mona sighed. She hadn't resigned herself to the fact that Alex did everything calmly. He had chosen a casket for their daughter calmly. Committed the final mitzvah—piling dirt on Libby's grave—calmly. Existed calmly. Even in the face of leaving their first home and especially in the face of leaving Libby's only home, Alex was calm.

"I hate your stoicism," Mona said. Her voice a whisper. "How can you possibly be so calm?"

The walls were lined with neatly packed cardboard boxes—a literal lifetime. Mona stroked the elephant again, but she wanted to rip its head off. She wanted to hear the satisfying sound of torn cloth. She didn't, though. It had been Libby's favorite thing. Its fur impossibly soft. She ran her thumb over the tag. The words "Lincoln Park Zoo" reminded her that she would have to go back to work soon. Was she able to care for animals after losing her only child?

Alex pressed his hand against Mona's shoulder, bringing her back.

"Libby deserved stoicism, didn't she?" he asked.

"No," Mona answered. "Libby deserved a life. Love. College. Normal.

Libby deserved normal."

"She did," Alex said. "But you don't always get what you deserve. She needed you while she was here. And you just couldn't…." His voice tapered off, incapable or unwilling to finish the thought.

Mona shrunk into herself, her shoulders shoved forward and her arms wrapped tightly across her chest.

"Maybe she deserved a father who waited to kiss her good morning. Who was there when," she said.

"When what, Mona?" Alex said. "*When she died*. You can't even say it. Half her life, you couldn't love her, and now that she's gone, you're the only one suffering?"

Alex paced the room, clenching his fist until his nails bit through his palm. Mona watched the terse trek, scared to leave but satisfied that he'd finally reached her level, lost control. She could feel his eyes burning into the side of her face. She resisted the urge to check her watch. His steps made loud thuds despite Alex's bare feet. They were like thunderclaps in the middle of a quiet evening. Mona fingered the eyelet curtains, refusing to really look at Alex.

"I was bored and scared. I didn't know myself anymore," she said.

She wanted to continue. To tell him how claustrophobic the post-partum felt. Like she looked in the mirror and some stranger was looking back at her. Like the gulps of air before a tidal wave drags you under.

"I tried to change, to get better."

Mona didn't know if that was the entire truth though. Things are rarely that simple. She honestly believed Libby lead her through the fog post-partum produced. Taking her hand and slowly convincing Mona that she was a mother. That happened in death though. People take on a mystical quality, immortalized in perfection.

"It's just easier for you. Your entire relationship was easy. You always wanted to hold her. You never screamed or left when she cried. You didn't have to find her."

"Easy," he said, still pacing in tight circles around the small room. "You think any of this is fucking easy for anyone?"

He pushed a stack of books from Libby's nightstand, and they bounced and cascaded across the wood floor. *Goodnight Moon, Pat the Bunny, A Sick Day for Amos McGee,* and *The Giving Tree* clattered against one another like a disorganized drum roll.

"When they cut her from you, they handed her to me." He paused. "When you weren't there. When you couldn't hold her, I held her. I fed her bottles. She cried for me," he said.

Mona felt the C-section scar along her abdomen. The raised flesh felt like a long welt, a belt lash branding her skin. She touched her tender breasts, engorged with milk. Slowly, the sticky liquid leaked onto her grey cotton t-shirt, circling her nipples.

"I don't care whose she was," Mona said with a resigned sigh. "She's gone now." Mona slid to the floor and rested her back against the purple walls. She held her knees to her chest, gazed sideways at Alex.

"I don't want to fight," she said. "I just want to be near someone who knew her. Someone who loved her better than I did."

Alex bent before her and rested his forehead against hers. They stayed that way until they heard the footsteps of movers.

Mona sipped the tea slowly. Allowed it to dribble across her tongue as she tried to enjoy the bitter taste. When she was young, Mona couldn't be blasted from bed. But late in Libby's life, the two of them had fostered a routine that made the daybreak hours endearing. While Alex started his day at the office, Mona woke early and changed Libby, nursed her leisurely, snuggled in bed. She didn't have to be in for rounds at the zoo until nine and Libby would wake at six, giving them three undisturbed hours of hazy happiness.

Now, she spent each morning hooked to the breast pump and listening to the droning "er…er…er…" of the machine's rhythm. She was producing less milk but the process of drying up was slow and painful. The veins in her breast ached, pulsing blue and vicious.

Mona was glad Alex had found an apartment with a different route to the zoo. She wouldn't have to ride the same bus she took Libby on. She wouldn't have to smell the same hot dogs from Weiner Circle as she passed. She wouldn't have to hear the same street music from the saxophonist who played on the corner of Clark. She didn't have to pass Libby's daycare center with the fluorescent art in the window. The bright sign that read Little Green Treehouse.

But today, she was going back to work. The night before, Mona received a call from her supervisor, Katherine. Mona and Alex had been relaxing after dinner, two glasses of Scotch and piles of backlogged work between them. Before Libby died, Mona had artificially inseminated an elephant named Evie who was overdue for a prenatal checkup.

"Mona," Katherine said, her voice high and nasally. "I know we said two weeks, but I was wondering if you could possibly come in sooner?"

Mona paused. She hadn't showered in a few days and her long brown hair was forming dreads without the benefits of shampoo and a brush. She thought about sawing the tangled mess off with a steak knife.

"Are you there?"

"Is everything ok?" Mona asked.

"Evie needs a detailed exam and she has a preference for you. But if you're not up to it, I can certainly have Mark take care of it."

Mark and Mona were friendly without the benefits of real loyalty. Like everyone in the field, Mark was competitive and outgoing and eager to step into the head vet role. Mona hated that he prioritized his career over the animals' best interests.

"I'd be happy to come in," Mona said.

Alex crinkled his forehead, looked up from a stack of briefs. She shrugged as if to say *what else do I have to do?* He flipped another page, though it seemed clear he hadn't finished the previous one. Katherine paused. Stagnant awkwardness grew between them like moss on a moist rock.

"San Diego made an offer on the calf," Katherine said.

"And Evie?" Mona asked quickly.

"Just the calf," Katherine said. "You know we don't really have the space—"

"Then why did we inseminate Evie?" Mona interrupted. *Don't cry*—she reminded herself. *Don't you dare cry.* She chewed on the inside of her lower lip.

"Mona, you know how zoos work."

*And why people despise them*, Mona thought as she clicked off the phone and looked over at Alex.

"I'm going in to see Evie tomorrow. Just Evie. It won't be a full day."

Alex hadn't returned to work at his family law firm yet. Mona knew he wouldn't for a while, too comatose with grief to focus.

"Are you ready for that?" Alex asked.

"I need to take care of Evie," Mona answered. "Just Evie," she repeated and thought about the sweet animal who loved lemonade and Libby.

***

Five months prior, Mona hadn't felt like anyone's mother. Libby's cries grated and bounced against her. She struggled to get Libby to latch to her breast and flinched as Libby dug her crescent-shaped infant nails into her flesh. The children's books that lined the walls were dull, and she couldn't force herself to read them aloud. The room smelled of piss and sweat, a smell that butchered Libby's baby scent. Mona's body felt like broken flab. It didn't move the way it once had. Her thighs chafed against one another, and her stomach resembled an old man's face. Her arms were constantly tired from holding Libby, rocking her, caring for her. Mona fought the instinct to run.

Then, towards the end of her maternity leave, Mona introduced Libby to her world at the zoo. It was early in the morning before crowds arrived, when the sun wouldn't scorch their necks. Mona walked through the gates to the elephant enclosure, using her clearance as the head vet in this one instance.

Trees curved and cast shadows over mud holes where four female elephants rested. The air smelled of manure and hay and stale popcorn. Mona called Evie into the barn behind the display—clicking her tongue and snapping her fingers.

She had brought a thermos of sweet lemonade. She carefully unscrewed the lid, allowing Evie's meticulous trunk to inhale the sticky treat in a few loud gulps. Mona didn't tie Evie to the stake despite the elephant's towering frame. She stood in her shadow, so close they were breathing the same air. Evie ran her trunk up and down Mona and Libby, scanning their bodies. The baby's eyes were wide with awareness, focused and attentive on the beautiful beast. The elephant used the two fingers inside her trunk to caress Libby's foot, her pink toes the size of acorns. Libby giggled lightly as Evie tickled her. The sound was soft and unimposing. Libby reached out a hand, straining away from Mona, and flattened her palm against Evie's brown hide. As she touched the elephant, the sound of Libby's laugh enveloped them as if it were a wave slowly carrying them away. Evie trumpeted, a loud burst that Mona had only heard elephant calves make.

Mona wanted to bathe in the noises, washing away the banal existence she'd had with Libby until then. She buried her face into the spongy spot between Libby's ear and her neck. She kissed it softly and memorized her scent. Mona brushed her lips against Evie's back with an exaggerated smacking sound before releasing her back into the pen. Mona felt certain this was a turning point. For the first time since becoming a mother, she felt whole. The love she had for Libby spread over her like the sun warming an errant patch of snow. Mona marched to the gift shop and bought Libby a stuffed elephant to commemorate their day. Her daughter combed it over her face, soothed by the fluff on its back. She turned it over, presented it to Mona, allowed her mother to snuggle it against her cheek before handing it back.

After that, the post-partum continued—a dull slog that would sneak up behind her. But it lessened. A faded blue rather than the darkest black night. Mona no longer wanted to flee.

The medical tent, as the staff at the zoo called it, was a towering weathered barn with heated cement floors at the northern end of the property. It held five long stalls big enough for the largest animals. Each stall was separated by insulated walls to block sound and prevent panic. Mona sat on a rolling stool so that she could easily access Evie's legs. She held four long syringes between her fingers, turning herself into the veterinary Freddy Kruger. The needles used to draw Evie's blood were nearly twelve inches long and felt cumbersome in Mona's hand. Evie was standing, tethered to the ground with a chain attached to a stake, shifting her weight from one leg to the other. Mona calmed her, talking softly about the weather as Katherine lightly stroked Evie's chest. In the past, the elephants were drugged with a dart gun. Thankfully, that practice had fallen out of favor.

Evie's demeanor changed to near stillness as Mona spoke. Slowly, Mona eased the first needle into the elephant's leg. She pulled the plunger back, and Evie moaned softly, presumably in discomfort. Mona had drawn blood from elephants hundreds of times. Still, the force necessary to pierce the skin always surprised her, like the kickback on a gun after it's fired. Katherine readied a blue caddy so that she could easily take the tubes of blood to the clinic in the zoo's main building.

"What's Mark's day look like?" Mona asked. She plunged another needle into Evie's leg. With each puncture, the elephant got more agitated, pawing the ground lightly to signal her displeasure.

"Kala, the anteater, has skin abrasions," Katherine said. "Then he's got to examine the newest bear cubs and anesthetize a python."

"Big day," Mona said.

"Then, of course, he'll help analyze this blood sample and sit in on my conference call with San Diego."

Mona pivoted on the chair so that she could see Katherine's face. The full vial hung from her left hand.

"I never would've inseminated Evie if you told me about the transfer. You knew that, right?" Mona asked.

"I called you as a courtesy, Mona. You're close to Evie. You've been through a lot."

Mona bit her lower lips, sucking in air hard. Katherine wore a condescending smirk, her eyebrows angled in an aggressive V.

"Have you ever heard the sound an elephant makes when she's upset?" Mona asked.

Katherine fiddled with the vials of blood—lifting them from the blue plastic carrying case and swirling them in the sunlight that shone through the barn's wall of windows.

"I studied African elephants with the IUCN for three years after I graduated," Mona began. "We were tracking a large female herd with strange migrant patterns. Every month or so they'd return to the same spot."

Katherine clicked her tongue lightly. Mona knew it was a signal that she should hurry the story along.

"When the elephants were there, the matriarch of the herd made this noise, a wail. A scream. The only thing I can compare it to are the sounds a woman makes in labor combined with the heart-wrenching cries of devastation."

"What was it?" Katherine asked.

"Two guides went and examined the grounds to see. There were elephant bones there. Small elephant bones in a shallow grave. We could only assume it was a burial site for her baby."

"You understand we're not harming the calf?"

Mona laughed quietly and smoothed the wrinkles on her forehead.

"Calves nurse for three years. The males live with their mother for twelve years or until he reaches puberty. The daughter," Mona stopped. "The daughter never leaves."

"I'm aware," Katherine said.

"My point is that your version of harm and mine are vastly different."

Mona stood and walked to the corner where she'd left Evie's chart. She leaned against the small folding table and filled in a few blanks on the form, signing her name in slanted script at the bottom.

"Have Mark analyze the progesterone levels for elevation and irregularities," Mona said. "My notes about her previous levels are in a file in the main building. In five months, we'll monitor Evie's serum prolactin levels as well. If I were you, I'd wait until then to broker your deal."

Mona strode from the barn, thinking of the cries from the African elephant. Of Evie and her new calf. She rubbed her temples, fighting a headache. She wanted to save her friend, Evie, from the heartache. Mona knew it was silly to think of Evie that way but it was a naked and undeniable truth. Mona had lost a daughter, and now Evie's daughter would be stripped from her, fed with a bottle rather than her mother's teat. Some part of that equation made Mona feel less alone but also, deeply sad. For so long she felt she had absorbed all the heartbreak in the world. Now she longed to prevent it.

Mona wanted to quit, but Evie kept drawing her back. Evie struggled with her equilibrium as she gained weight. She would stumble and fall when it rained. One morning, during a thunderstorm, Mark couldn't get her into the barn. Evie was afraid to cross a muddy pit. She refused to have her blood drawn a few times. Wouldn't lift her leg for foot care. She responded to Mona alone.

In return, Mona advocated for her. She sparred with Katherine. She brought in statistics about emotional damage to elephants. She spoke to experts researching African elephants in the wild. She contacted a sanctuary in Tennessee, desperate to find a place for Evie and her calf.

"Retire her," Mona said, cornering Katherine on a Monday when visitation was low. They were walking through the flamingo forest, pink feathers floating from the trees like gently falling snow.

"Retire Evie?" Katherine said. "That's a joke, right?"

"Retire her and retire the calf and let them live in the wild."

Katherine's mouth hung open, her eyes unable to focus on anything. "Evie was born in captivity. She couldn't adapt."

"Fine. Then a sanctuary. A reserve. Or transfer them both to San Diego. Just don't separate them. You can't."

Mona's words ran together. She reached out to grasp Katherine's shoulder, to turn her around so she could read Mona's desperation. But Katherine was too fast. Katherine pivoted as she entered the zoo's main offices, pressed the door open with her back.

"Those elephants are our biggest draw. They're the zoo's most popular exhibit and as such, they raise money. They ensure we can continue to offer free admission. Evie was born here." She paused. "Drop. This. Now," Katherine said, poking at the air. Mona watched Katherine disappear in the row of offices, her shoulders pressed back and hair glistening. There was a confidence in her strut, an unending determination that Mona envied.

Mona walked to Evie's pen. The elephant lay behind a thick log with her back to the crowds. Her belly was hard and round. She had been pregnant a year and still had ten months to go. Mona remembered that point in her pregnancy when she was so uncomfortable, moving hurt. Her ankles swollen. Sweat under her stomach pooling and chafing. Her back in tight knots. Mona ran her fingers against the bars. She hated being pregnant. She hated the way her personal space was consistently invaded by friends and family and the occasional stranger as they stroked her tummy. How a bizarre combination of cravings and morning sickness would ruin her day. She despised feeling like a vessel as Alex continually asked what she ate and drank and did. How his gaze felt accusatory as she told him a ham sandwich, one that wasn't warmed to fight listeria. As Mona stared at Evie struggling to stand, she knew she never wanted to be pregnant again.

Mona thought of Alex and how tentative he was when he first told her he wanted to have a child. They had been in the bedroom of their old apartment on Sheridan Road and he had lightly traced her shoulders, the pads of his fingers delicate like a ripple on a pond. *Let's start a family*, he'd said in a voice that was part man, part purr. The moment had excited her, before she understood the sacrifices and the risks.

Alex had reached for her recently. His fingers traveled from her lower back and inner thighs. He wanted her to consider having another child. The thing she couldn't say aloud was that she had a child. She had the only child she wanted to have.

"I'm not ready," she said to him, grasping his hand as it trailed along her body and pulling it on top of their blue and cream duvet. Alex smoothed the covers as he tried to avoid Mona's eyes.

"Do you think—" Alex stopped. "Do you think you will be soon?"

"What's the question exactly?" Mona asked. "Is it, are you ready to have sex? Or, are you ready to have another baby?"

"Both."

Mona twirled a loose strand of hair around her pointer finger. She pretended to scratch her shoulder—an excuse to hug herself more tightly.

"Can we talk about this later? It's really a bad time."

Alex propped himself up on his right elbow and fingered the papers on Mona's lap. Mona leaned her head against their padded headboard, her eyes fixated on the ceiling. Alex rolled over and lit a cigarette, holding it in a pucker between his lips.

"I know we need to talk," she began. She grabbed his free hand, rubbed the peaks and valleys of his knuckles with her thumb. She fought the urge to cry, squeezing his hand a few quick times. Alex undoubtedly noticed the tears that seeped from her. He nodded towards the black files with Evie's medical records and Mona's research.

"How's it going?" he asked, blowing the smoke away from her.

Mona looked at the files on her lap, then at her husband. She had known Alex for ten years. She'd built a family and lost one with him. He'd seen her graduate vet school. They'd lived in five different apartments. She knew in the morning he ate almonds. She could predict the book he would buy in an airport as they rushed to their gate. Still, knowing him didn't help her explain anything. She stared up at his face, memorizing the new lines that streaked across his forehead.

Mona laced her fingers through his, resting her temple on his shoulder. She wanted to tell him how important Evie was to her. At the same time, she needed him to know that she couldn't be a mother again. The title was permanently shucked from her like some form of karmic punishment.

"I don't know what to do," Mona said. She looked up at him. She wanted to add more, unsure if the comment was about his desire for more children or about Evie or both. She let the words float in the air with the lingering cigarette smoke.

\*\*\*

Later that week, Katherine called in the middle of the night. Evie was making a loud, alarming noise. It echoed throughout the zoo, causing the other animals to chatter deafeningly to one another. When Mona arrived, she heard the squawks of the flamingos, the deep roar of the lions, the restless groan of the trees as the apes swung aggressively through the branches. It was a symphony, and Evie's painful cry underscored the rhythm.

The air was unseasonably cool and a thin layer of dew rested on the ground. The three other elephants in the herd had been removed from the pen. Evie was alone. The lights were bright, but Evie was in a shady grove by a tree line. As Mona got closer, she noticed Evie was bent over a small, immobile lump. The calf was a deep gray color—a combination of its natural hue and the blood from delivery. Evie's trunk was wrapped around her baby's stomach. Even with her experience in Africa, Mona had never heard a sound as fresh and raw as Evie's bawl. She thought back to the day she had discovered Libby, her chest no longer rising and falling. Her skin tinged blue. Somewhere within her, Mona knew she'd made a sound like Evie's. The wails were long and low, sorrowful.

"Evie?"

Evie lifted her head, suspicious of anyone who encroached on her and her daughter.

"Evie, it's ok. I don't want to hurt you. I don't want to hurt her."

Mona made herself smaller; she got on her knees and crawled the remaining distance between them. There was a rim around the elephant's eyes that looked strange, like bright blue eye shadow. Her eyelashes were highlighted by moist condensation. She couldn't stop crying.

Mona laid her hand on the calf's side. Even wildly premature, the calf would weigh over one hundred pounds.

"She's beautiful, Evie," Mona said. She remembered her own daughter's birth. The cold, sterile room. The white blinding lights. The shrieking wail of life filled with hope rather than pain. "She's really special."

Evie cried again and Mona wanted to carry her away. She wanted to take her some place to be alone, to grieve. Instead, she sat with Evie and the dead calf. Mona collected a few branches that had peeled from the trees nearby, leaning and stretching her fingers so that she wouldn't have to get up and startle Evie. Mona stacked the brittle twigs, two or three layers high, around the calf's body in a tight square. She thickened the lines with pine needles that were nearly the same texture, brown and stiff. Evie stared intently at Mona as she worked. Then, the elephant followed suit—extending her trunk and breaking a limb from a thin tree nearby. They encircled the stillborn with a casket and laid just outside the makeshift box, gazing at the baby Evie had created. The one she lost.

Mona pushed through the door after an hour. Katherine waited in the barn. She had a nervous habit of chewing on her nails, and she aggressively worked on her pinkie. There was blood on Mona's hands and down her jeans. She smelled like mud and pennies. She started washing her hands. The water scalded her stained skin, causing them to flush pink again. She was unable to speak.

"Well," Katherine said, her voice sharp as she came closer to Mona. "What happened?"

Mona stopped, ran her hand over her eyes, and lightly scratched her jawline. When she was uncomfortable, tiny hives formed at the base of Mona's face and she felt raised bumps as they corroded her skin. She dried her hands even though they were still tarnished with Evie's blood.

"Stillborn. And that elephant." She paused. "That elephant will never be the same."

"What can we—?" Katherine began.

"Just stop." Mona slammed her arms against the sink, the paper towel clenched in her fist. "Let her go. Let her go anywhere else. Let her have a life outside."

Katherine's arms were crossed defensively and her mouth was a thin, definitive line.

"There's space at a sanctuary in Tennessee. Let Evie retire there. Please."

Mona sounded like a petulant child as she begged. She crossed her ankles and looked at the cheaply paneled ceiling.

Mona sighed. "My kid looked like that, Katherine, and I had to figure out what to do. Before I really knew how to be her mother, I had to bury her."

Katherine didn't say anything. She scurried around the room, stacking and rearranging files in a flurry of nervous energy. Mona crossed the floor and touched her forearm, a way of calming her.

"You have a son, right?"

Katherine nodded her head slowly.

"Now imagine you don't. He's gone. You wouldn't want to be in the same space. Can you hear Evie wailing? If she stays here, she'll die of a broken heart. I can see that happening. Please. It's an extenuating circumstance. Please let us take the spot in the sanctuary."

Katherine was unable to speak, her lips forming words that didn't come out. Mona imagined she was picturing the terrifying scenes that go through all mothers' minds. The glimpses of anxiety and worry that accompany every skinned knee and broken bone. All late night phone calls when their children have missed curfew. That burning question that lingers. What if I can't protect them? Mona gently rubbed Katherine's back, the slideshow in her mind conjuring Libby's lifeless body.

***

Two weeks later, Mona chose a quiet spot to bury the remains of Evie's daughter. It was on a slight incline within the sanctuary's one hundred and twenty acres. The eastern perimeter was lined with mango trees, and Evie had eaten so many within her first week at The Farm, her fecal matter had turned fluorescent orange. Evie visited the tiny grove daily and lingered there well past dusk when the sun hung so close to the ground it looked like low-hanging fruit.

The groundskeeper had dug a shallow grave in preparation for the burial. It was a grave that would easily be uncovered. Alex stood next to Mona, wearing a plain white t-shirt and khaki shorts. The two had driven the calf's ashes and a few small bones removed from the calf's foot in a simple pine box to the sanctuary's grounds. The bones would help Evie stop and recognize and mourn, her sense of smell able to easily detect her daughter's remains.

"Have you ever heard of a sky burial?" Alex asked.

"No," Mona replied.

"It's this. It's what we're doing. You bury your loved ones at the top of a hill. You allow them to be exposed to the elements. To the animals. You let nature take its course."

"What about visiting? Talking to them?" Mona asked. She remembered Alex placing black seashells on Libby's grave, remnants of a recent vacation. He had mourned in the cemetery, visiting often to replace flowers and clean Libby's headstone. Mona found no peace in that place but sometimes she would buy pink balloons and, standing at her grave, she would send them into the air, picturing her bubbly girl extending her hand to graze one.

"Do you think the only place you can talk to Libby is a grave?" he said. He removed the elephant calf's cremated ashes, scattering them into the hole and sifting sand around them. Then Mona placed the few bones Evie would uncover just below the surface of the grave, an ecru slice jutting from the earth. "Libby's everywhere. I see her in everything. Sometimes I think I hear her laugh in the next room or on a bus. It's like a phantom limb," he said.

Mona sat on the ground beside the grave. She wrenched her knees to her chest, hugging them tightly as she rested her chin on them.

"I sing to her sometimes," Mona said. "That awful Barney song about family. I smack my lips together after the line *with a kiss from me to you*. Just the way I did when she was alive."

An elephant walked behind Alex. She used her trunk to pry the tall braided grass from the ground. It was Tia, the African matriarch. She was forty-four years old, retired from the circus. Her hide was puckered with hook wounds. They looked like round track marks, each a perfect circle highlighted by raised skin.

"I wish I could've done anything right."

Alex dusted the clay and the ashes from his hands. He sat down beside her and rested his forearm against the small of her back.

"We can try again," he said, half-heartedly.

"No," Mona said simply. "I can't."

She picked the dirt from her nails.

"Do you have a cigarette?" she asked. He shook one out of a new pack, held a Zippo lighter to the end. The tip glowed orange in front of her. She hadn't smoked in years but at this moment, something about the smell made her feel more like her. More at home. She didn't take a drag. She let it burn to her fingertips.

"You look at home," Alex said, leaning casually against a thick tree trunk. His tone wasn't laced with anger, the way it once had been. Mona smiled.

"I like it here," she said.

"You're not coming back, are you?" Alex asked, cutting through the chitchat.

Mona looked down at her shoes. She watched Tia and wished she could run her hands along her skin, excavating the physical pain.

"I think this is where I should be."

"I thought you might say that."

Alex stood and looped his pointer finger through his belt loop. He towered over Mona until she climbed to her feet with a grunt, facing him. He pulled her to him, smelling her hair. Mona heard another elephant moving through the grove. It was Evie. She played with a deflated soccer ball nearby, watching Alex and Mona. A jubilance exuded from her as she high-stepped through the course straw.

"Stay with me," Mona said, placing her hand on his elbow.

Alex shuffled his feet, knocking over his red backpack. On it was an enamel pin of an elephant and the sanctuary's name.

"I want another baby," he said bluntly. "I want to choose the first song my kid hears and get up at three a.m."

"I think I'll always look for Libby in any baby we have," Mona said.

Alex pigeon-toed his feet then rubbed the sole of his shoe against his calf. He slipped his hand into the side pocket of the bag and pulled out the impossibly soft elephant with the words "Lincoln Park Zoo" on its tag.

"I know you give yourself hell," he said. "But you were a good mom."

Mona scrubbed the stuffed animal over her eyes, wiping the tears. She inhaled deeply, smelling Libby.

# They Always Wave Goodbye

THE black circle was printed on heavy, off-white cardstock. In West Virginia, the paper had been thin and waxy. The clinic in Charleston had straight-back chairs and windows so high you couldn't see the lingering signs of the Chinese restaurant next door. But the Thomson Clinic in Chicago had wide leather chairs aged intentionally to look antique. It had a wall of windows and a coffee bar. It smelled like handpicked lemons, not synthetic like lemon air freshener. Annie breathed easier as her father, William, took the test, confident they had made the right choice in seeking a second opinion.

"The circle is a clock," the clinician said, intruding on Annie's thoughts. "Please write in the numbers." Annie watched the woman start a stopwatch and take a seat beside her, facing William's back. William dried his hands on his pleated khakis before beginning the test. Annie remembered thirty-five years ago when he was on the team to build the New River Gorge Bridge. Six months into the bridge's construction, he was hauled up the rust-colored sides in an oversized bucket. During the ascent, she'd watch him dry his hands on his thick, worn jeans, removing the only physical sign of his nerves.

This was the third time he'd taken the clock test to evaluate the level of his mind's deterioration and each result veered further from normal. It always started the same way. Fill in the numbers. William could get that part easily. He was a mechanical engineer. Making things work was part habit, part calling. William tapped his pen on the table. Annie remembered science projects he'd built for her, including a hydrographic activator. She recalled a music box reworked to play "Heart and Soul" after she learned to play it on the piano. Drawing a clock shouldn't stymie her dad. He could fix engines, design a drainage system, build a bridge 876 feet tall.

William pressed his fingers to his temples in an attempt to Jedi mind trick the simple information. He scratched his palms and looked around, but the room was shucked free of distractions. William started to write, the pen moving so aggressively the table wobbled. The writing was a slow and agitated scratch. The clinician peered over William's shoulder. William swatted absentmindedly as if she was a gnat. The woman reset the clock and Annie exhaled, feeling certain William had passed the first portion.

"Now, draw the minute and hour hands at ten after eleven," the woman said, her voice echoing against the walls. William sighed loudly, exhaling exasperation.

This was where trouble typically arose. Her father's brain, once able to calculate the area of concrete in his head, now confused ten after and ten 'til. Annie couldn't stop her mind from whirling through all the things he'd taught her. She helped him install a shower once. His rough, calloused hands capably connecting and conjoining smooth silver pipes. His mouth puckered in a whistle. Because of him, she knew how to change a tire, install a garbage disposal, apply wallpaper. She knew how to bait a hook, pushing on the worm's midsection so the head swelled before piercing the slimy creature behind the swollen band. She could determine the best docks for bluegills at Plum Orchard Lake. Annie once thought this was what a man should be. She adored him through lost years. Years when he embarrassed her. Years when they had little if anything in common. Years when he thought his prayers could absolve her sexuality. She defended him despite his disapproval of her life. She loved him but feared she didn't know him.

Annie remembered the expression, *A son's a son until he finds a wife, a daughter's a daughter all of her life.* It was an odd thing to remember because it wasn't William's expression but her mother's nasal voice, weighed down with her accent and the Marlboro Light propped at the edge of her mouth. Her mother, Samantha, who could make gourmet food, occasionally rolling out puff pastry dough that would envelop steak, allowing the rich aroma of Beef Wellington to float seamlessly through the one-story house. Her mother, who never worked outside their home, preferring the sanctuary of her prize-winning hydrangeas. Her mother, who thought traditional values meant submissively backing from an argument to flip her father off in the adjoining room. Her mother, whose car jumped a guardrail in the middle of a sunny June day, killing her on impact when Annie was twenty.

Samantha was full of these colloquialisms, and they played on a tape in Annie's mind. The day before, Annie had told her son, Georgie, *she was going to slap both eyes into one* because *he was too big for his britches.* She had stopped to look around, expecting her mother to appear with a shit-eating grin and a cigarette needing to be ashed.

The clinician, her hair twirled into a tight bun, snapped Annie back to reality as she clicked off the stopwatch. She retrieved the page from William and scribbled notes directly on it. Annie stole a peek, could see her father had gotten the minute hand correct but there was no hour hand. A few of the numbers on the edge were missing. Knowledge her father had for sixty years had evaporated.

\*\*\*

Annie and William hadn't seen Dr. Travers after the testing but as she drove them home, she imagined what the doctor would say, stroking his slim moustache. *The dementia is progressing quickly. He needs routine.* Annie shook her head, trying to free the doubt that clouded it. She navigated into her parking spot, sandwiched between a smart car and a red VW Beetle. Annie carried in an oversized briefcase brimming with manuscripts and balanced a sack of groceries on her hip. William cracked his knuckles, fixated on his own thoughts. He didn't offer to help. As they scurried into the townhouse, Annie tossed her keys on a lacquered console and started unloading the groceries. She wanted to focus on dinner and playtime and work but she couldn't shake the test from her memory. Annie hoped the decisions she made for her dad were best.

Her father was Appalachian, as much a part of the mountains as the soil, the maples Annie used to scale, the bluegills she and her father threw back in the lake. He never wanted to leave, even as the disease chewed through his central nervous system, but Annie and Georgie wanted him here. Annie wanted to take her dad to Millennium Park and stand beneath the Bean's mirrored surface, smell the metal, and admire the Chicago skyline, the architecture. She wanted him to taste the kick from the peppers on a Chicago dog at Weiner Circle. She wanted him to help Georgie catch a foul ball at Wrigley Field. She needed him to understand why she left. She needed him to see that somewhere else could be home. Somewhere else could produce the siren call West Virginia had, could seduce you, nurture you, love you. She needed him to see this even if her dreams were filled with the oranges and golds of the trees in autumn, her ears consumed with the high-pitched train whistle that hugged the mountain curves, her mouth filled with the taste of deer jerky from Whipple General Store.

Again, her mother's voice rattled against her, taking her to the day her mother and father hugged Annie when they were leaving her in Morgantown. Her mother with deep mascara lines gliding towards her chin, kissing both Annie's cheeks, sliding Annie's auburn hair behind her ears. *You have to wave goodbye. Children always wave goodbye.* That felt like both a lie and the truth. Annie had left West Virginia but she couldn't rinse it from her. Her mother had left this earth but she could be conjured. Her father was still here sometimes, still himself in the quiet but displaced moments. Annie didn't want to wave goodbye.

She tried to focus on the papers splayed across her L-shaped couch as Georgie and William built a tall Lego tower. They alternated wide green and blue bricks at the base; the upper layers were all red. Annie watched the two of them as their construction progressed. She loved Georgie's curved spine, the way his brows formed a straight line when he concentrated. With his blond hair and cowlicks and one dimple—just one—on the right side, as if someone declared, *cute enough—one more dimple might throw things off balance,* Georgie looked like William. Georgie kicked over the Lego tower with a grunt that was burrowed in his belly. William avoided the plastic shrapnel and started collecting the blocks in one wide hand. "Samantha," he said, looking earnestly at Annie but mistaking her for her mother. "Annie has the worst temper."

They sat in the silence that followed. William looked down at his exposed toes and blinked twice. He'd always recognized his family. The slip, mistaking Annie for her mom and Georgie for Annie, was momentary. It could have been shrugged away as old age, but Annie committed it to memory, recognizing how lost her father truly was.

Georgie snuggled into William's arms. "Georgie," her son said, pointing to his skinny six-year-old body and making Annie laugh. Georgie allowed the prickles on William's chin to tickle his neck as they sat transfixed, looking at nothing. They lingered that way, folded in a slumped L, until it was time for dinner. Annie thrust chicken nuggets and French fries and too much ketchup on a plate. Georgie taught William to use the nuggets as a ketchup shovel. Both had stains on the cuffs of their shirts but Annie reveled in the dinner and in the ease Georgie's constant prattle produced.

"You never shut up either," William said at one point and Annie only nodded, unwilling to wade through her childhood as the dementia amputated her father's future.

From there, Annie felt William deteriorating further each day. He didn't get lost, didn't meander into traffic, or think his underwear was a hat. He didn't do the silly things you think happen in the early days of dementia. It was more about his inability to place himself. As Annie drove along Lake Shore Drive, William read the billboards aloud.

"Don't text and drive," William said in a booming voice, startling Annie whose mind was wandering to the cookies she needed to buy for Georgie's class. "Nightlife included, Pure Michigan."

William's eyes were staring out the side window, his fingers tracing the outline of a billboard they were about to pass. "You are beautiful," he said. It was written on a plain white sign in oversized black letters. The font was simple. It advertised nothing. William's voice sounded low, meticulous, and romantic. A soothing strum mingling with his traditional baritone. The change in his tone frightened Annie. He picked up her hand from the gearshift. "You really are, Samantha," he said and kissed her palm, allowing his pursed lips to linger above Annie's pale freckled wrist. She wriggled her hand free from his firm grasp, awkwardly fingered the split ends of her hair.

"It didn't mean anything," he said urgently. "She wasn't you."

The gridlocked traffic buzzed around them. Horns blared as they progressed slowly. Annie focused on sliding her foot from the brake to the gas and back again.

"Daddy," she said trying to focus on the ebb and flow of traffic but yearning to reach out and touch his shoulder, rub his back, a gesture that felt familiar to their relationship. She wanted to hug him like he had hugged her when she fell from her two-wheel bike. To support him as he had when her mother died—Annie's back clad in a wool dress that itched, a dress she chose because she never wanted to wear it again, a dress she picked so she could bury it in the bottom of a Goodwill donation bin.

"Daddy," Annie repeated. "You know I'm Annie. I'm your ...."

She was going to say daughter.

"Squirrel," he said, filling in her blank with a nickname he hadn't called her in years. Not since she came out to him.

Annie was nineteen when she told her parents. Her first girlfriend had been a petite blond named Kim who wore button-downs secured at the collar and bracelets that moved rhythmically against one another in a cacophonous symphony. It was Christmas break, and she was home from school. The air was tight with the prospect of snow and the smell of pine needles. Samantha had baked an apple pie, and the smell and the nerves together turned Annie's stomach. Her father built a fire, stoking the embers with a long iron poker.

"I met someone at school," Annie said, her voice shaking against the words. William didn't stop. The wood made a loud grinding clatter.

"That's nice, Squirrel," he said, distractedly. "You going to bring him by? Maybe for New Year's?"

"It's a she," Annie said, softly.

"What's that?" her mother asked, shuffling into the room in flimsy slippers and sitting the pie on the coffee table.

"I'm dating a woman," Annie repeated stiffly, nervous her parents would call her a homosexual, which felt clinical and forced and overwhelmingly p.c.

"Maybe don't bring her for dinner then," William replied with a quick chuckle that felt dismissive and comforting simultaneously. Annie didn't know if she should overreact, maybe shove the pie off the table or stomp away. Everything felt trite, so instead, she flipped through *Southern Living*. William watched the fire overtake the wood. He dried his hands on his pants, ignoring the chill emanating from the stone floors. He sat on the bench in front of the fireplace and ran a hand through his hair, exhaling as if trying to catch his breath. He stared in the glow of the fire for so long that, for a moment, Annie was sure he would throw himself into the flames.

"She's a nice person," Annie said, her voice a wobbly incline. The truth was Kim felt wild and adventurous and a little dangerous, like standing in the middle of the New River Gorge Bridge while coal trucks zoomed overhead. Like sipping Jack and Gingers instead of studying.

"We're just ... surprised," William said. He wouldn't look at her. Her mother cut the pie in fat slabs and went to stand behind William. Annie felt like they were a group of statues strategically placed so the aromatic cinnamon could swirl between them.

"I don't want you to be lonely," William said, his eyes soft.

Annie felt taken aback and confused and expectant. How could she be lonely? She had just told them she was dating. Her mother crossed the room and stood near her. She didn't hug her but the shadowed presence felt like support. Annie inspected her nail bed, paying close attention to hangnails in an attempt to suppress tears.

"Let's talk about this later," William said, poking the fire and avoiding eye contact. Annie didn't argue.

That evening, when they assumed she was asleep, Annie listened to them talk in the hushed whispers of intimacy. She stood outside their door like a child. There were muffled sobs Annie would connect to William. Her mother's voice claiming it might be an experiment, a phase, an act of rebellion. There was hope behind the phrases. She heard her mother tell him it was okay. Annie was still Annie.

"Normal," her father said, hiccupping slightly. "All you want for your kids is a nice normal life. She won't get that now. Not here at least." Annie swished this back and forth in her mind. To her father, she was abnormal.

On Christmas, a thin snow fell, and Annie rode with William to the New River Gorge Bridge. It was their tradition, the only time Annie really saw her father admire his work. They sat under the broad beams and watched two hawks circle the area, disappearing behind the gray sky only to reappear lower on the horizon. When she was young, Annie thought the bridge was a consistent rainbow, its underside a perfect arch and its sides gnawed on both sides by the mountains. The top, where cars passed, was the line in the horizon she looked for. The bridge's rusted beams pronounced against clear skies. Even in her dreams, Annie could hear the rapids below. The water clawing across the rocks and battering the yellow rafting boats.

"I feel like I don't know you anymore," William said. "What with your secret." Icy breaths released in a thin stream in front of him.

"I'm still me," Annie said, crushing a frozen piece of bark back and forth with the toe of her shoe. "Still Squirrel," she said, hopefully. Her father looked her over.

"No," he said. "It doesn't feel like that now." Something in his voice cracked.

The moment drained away, neither of them knowing what should be said next. Both of them silent and resilient and stubborn and alone.

Annie had other girlfriends, but she found her way back to Kim. They had a civil ceremony in Chicago. William walked her down the aisle. She wore a lace gown and Kim wore a tight mermaid dress that accentuated her thin frame. Annie kissed her dad at the end of the red carpeted aisle at the cheap Holiday Inn, but William wouldn't look at Kim when he released Annie to her. He didn't ask Kim to dance. He left before they cut the cake. When Annie and Kim decided Annie would carry Georgie, William expressed his relief that she was "the woman in the relationship." Following the insemination, when she was wide and ripe and glowing, her father was most at ease. He built her a rocking chair from an old oak tree in their back yard. Deer and rabbits, a bear and a cardinal were carved in the head, and the chair cradled Annie and Georgie during three o'clock feedings.

Four years later, when Annie got divorced, William's ease was palpable, a loosening in his shoulders. A spinster daughter was acceptable. A lesbian was harder to explain.

Annie thought of all the times he'd called her Squirrel. When he bought her books and wrote it in the upper left hand corner, a reminder of who the book belonged to. When she was scared of swimming and he coaxed her into the deep end with the promise of ice cream sandwiches. The list of times he'd spoken the word was both too long and too short. She'd ached for the name without realizing it.

Now, as the car idled on Lake Shore Drive, the word was heavy. It felt like a beating heart vibrating on her dashboard.

"Daddy," Annie said. "I'm not Mom." William nodded but didn't respond for a few moments. Horns blasted in the background.

"You remind me of her, Squirrel."

Annie bathed in the praise, in the name.

"What would you say if she were here?" William asked.

Annie rolled her earlobe back and forth between her thumb and forefinger as the cars picked up speed. "I don't know. What about you?"

"I'm sorry," he said, his voice softer and steadier still. "I cheated on her."

Annie momentarily wanted to cry for her mother who'd been undoubtedly hurt but her father garnered her sympathy too. That was a long time to carry so much guilt.

"Just once," William said, staring into his lap. "Not much consolation."

"No," Annie said. Her eyes bore into the license plate in front of her. It was from Iowa. William was looking out at the lake as rain beat the sand into mud. The boats clashed with the wooden docks like cubes in a cocktail. The view was lovely and tumultuous. They passed another billboard but William didn't read it aloud.

"I cheated on Kim once, too," Annie said, remembering a redhead and an office party and too many salty margaritas. She remembered the guilt that came afterwards like a bucket filled with icy water. She remembered imagining what she would tell Georgie. "Did Mom know?"

"Yes," William said softly. "She resented me for a long time. I never thought we would get through that. Then she died, and I just had myself to blame for all of it."

Annie looked out the window. Life was messy, she thought. Her mother was here and gone. Her father was here and gone. Her son was beautiful and smart and loved and he came from a syringe. Her best friend was her ex-wife. She wanted to be here. She missed West Virginia.

"Daddy," Annie said, the name almost a question in itself. "Should we go home?"

William's glance turned into a stare. Annie felt his eyes singe her cheeks and wiggled in the seat uncomfortably. He placed his hand on hers, rubbing his thumb back and forth the way he had a thousand times before. The gesture was an answer itself, a kindness that couldn't mend but eased her apprehensions.

Annie tried to make the move but obstacles—her job, her townhouse, visitation schedules with Kim—stood in the way. William asked about leaving. He watched Mountaineer basketball, March Madness, on the big screen in her living room, reciting names he remembered to Georgie. When he forgot players' names, he reincarnated players from the past. Willie Akers. Hot Rod Hudley. Jerry West. People Annie recognized from the days when she watched with him, sandwiched on the couch between he and her mother, as William did loud play-by-plays. At night, when Georgie went to bed, William filled the kitchen with the aromatic smells of chocolate-hinted coffee.

"Daddy, you should rest," Annie said, sitting in one of the mismatched kitchen chairs. She folded her legs underneath her.

"I don't want to talk in my sleep," William said, running a finger around the edge of his oversized, chipped mug.

"Why not?" Annie said. Georgie wandered into the room, groggily rubbing his eyes. He curled into William's lap.

"I don't want to lose anything else. When I sleep, more of the junk I used to know leaves."

Annie thought of their moment in the car and the return of her nickname. The way the words had calmed her, even following her father's confession about his infidelity. She understood why he would force himself to stay awake. To focus. To be here.

"When you told me you liked girls," William began, breathing harshly. Georgie flattened his hand on William's cheek. The action appeased him. "I felt betrayed because I thought I knew you. You told me and I was shocked. I mean, if I missed something that big, I had to have overlooked you. I didn't mean to."

Annie settled her hand over Georgie's. It was too late for all of them to be up and the darkness shrouded every part of the townhouse except their small corner.

"We love you," Georgie said in his too-loud, childish tone. Annie nodded, unable to move closer or further from them. They sat that way for a long time listening to the sound of taxi wheels against asphalt. Finally, as Georgie began to doze, Annie carried him to his room and slid him between his Justice League sheets. He snored lightly, spittle forming a small bubble at the corner of his mouth.

The next morning, Annie woke and couldn't find William until she looked outside. He was splayed on the grass in the courtyard in just tighty whiteys, his legs caked with the straw-like texture. *Skivvies*: the word popped against Annie's brain. It's what her mom called underwear when Annie was a girl with pink chubby rolls that cascaded down her thighs and puckered at her ankles. Her father still called them that when referencing Georgie's Underoos, the ones with Superman insignias and a red cotton waistband. The mowed lawn clung to her father's calves, green freckles dotting tan limbs. Blue veins merged with the blades of grass and snaked along his kneecaps.

"What's going on?" Georgie asked, his sleep interrupted by William's odd personality shift. William spread his limbs wide, up and down and up again.

"Snow angels," he hollered with a mania Annie didn't recognize. A wide grin was plastered across his face. It looked prosthetic.

Georgie scurried towards the fun, shedding the white t-shirt, the too long blue flannel pants. His body was thin, having just lost the last layer of baby fat but not yet achieving the muscles that t-ball and riding a 2-wheeler at the park would surely produce. The things he loved still had a babyish quality, though he wouldn't admit it. He clung to his tattered blankie and lullabies and the story *Goodnight Moon*. He liked to throw big fistfuls of change into the fountain at the mall. Quarters and pennies and dimes chinking together.

The two romped as the morning sun wicked away the last of the dew, naked except for their skivvies. One man old, wrinkled, memories seeping from him like oil expelling itself from a used car. There but not there, not all there. The other gaining something, picking this moment up like a toy, shiny and new in the cellophane wrapper. Committing to memory the time he and William made snow angels in the lawn as the sun lightly tickled their waxy skin.

Annie gazed out at the day. Men wheeled rickety recycling cans to the curb. They glimpsed towards her family then averted their eyes swiftly. But Annie refused to look away, preserving the playfulness that radiated from her father, the tangible happiness from her son.

"Squirrel," William called, waving rapidly.

Annie smiled and returned the wave.

## Ten Things

AFTER your mom died, when the eulogy had been delivered and the thank you notes written, you realized you knew her in a very specific way. That your love, while grand and all-consuming, was limited where hers was not. You begin to question your father and your sister and your mother's best friend on the details you aren't privy to, the molecules and the particles and the atoms that made up the person you wanted to know. Here are ten things you learned.

**Ten.** Your mother once wanted to be a writer. She sat, a pencil hovering above an empty page, looking longingly at the bareness. There were papers kept high in the closets of your parents' house. Scribbles and half-sentences brandished on the page, embossed in a hand-writing remarkably hers. She could neatly make an 'a' … the round circle and stick precise and meticulous, clearly two separate motions. When you were younger, you remember her writing letters to her friends, her sister, your father's mother—Nonie—who was in a home many hours away. She took such time with those notes. Careful to spell each word correctly, to make each letter legible. When she finished a paragraph, she would read it aloud to you, her voice proud and clear and even.

Your mother wrote about you. Every little girl in the stories you found had your curls. Each child had deep dimples and eyes with flecks of green. The girls in her stories are proud and stubborn. They slay dragons and swim across endless ocean expanses.

You think you have disappointed her with your ordinariness. You think she must have been bored with the everyday nature of your life, your marriage, your daughter, your work. You have an undeniable urge to do something adventurous and book a trip to Cape Cod. You take your daughter to the top of a lighthouse. The two of you lean over a railing and allow the ocean air to lick your faces. You close your eyes and imagine your mother is there, watching. Waiting. Writing. Something about the trip makes you feel better. Something about the trip makes you feel worse.

Your father tells you your mother never published anything but her friend uncovers a photocopy from a magazine. Your mother's name is at the top and there's a picture of you holding the family cat by its tail. The hair on its back stands on end and its body is a curved c desperately trying to claw its way up your arm to free itself. You're laughing in the photo. Your entire face a movement of muscles, your eyes squinted closed, your head thrown back with torrents of curls dangling like lifelines to drunken sailors. The story is an anecdote about you and as you read, you have two thoughts. It's well-written and you wish you had done more within it. Been better, funnier, original. The girl in the picture looks like an unstoppable force and you're jealous of the life she'll probably lead before you realize it's your own.

**Nine.** There was a moment in her pregnancy with you when a doctor asked her to have an abortion. When asked, your father didn't use the word abortion. He stared at the wrinkles permanently engraved on his hands as he explained the test. She was thirty-six and scared and they were calling her geriatric.

"She was wearing a pink blouse the day of the test," he said and, had you asked, you think he could've retrieved the blouse from her closet upstairs.

He wasn't allowed in the room but your mother told him they inserted a long needle into her uterus. She was worried about the needle, concerned it would puncture your skull. Your dad said Mom used to sing softly when she was scared. You remember that then. Recall her humming Sam Cooke's "Bring It On Home To Me" after she slammed her brakes and nearly crashed you into the wide backside of a school bus.

"She was mad. Indignant," Dad said. "I remember her singing softly for months afterwards."

You don't know what the doctors saw. You remembered your own tests when they held an ultrasound probe over the bump. Statistics rumbled through the air, bouncing off the walls around you. You cried when they told you Adeline was healthy, hugging your stomach hard with relief and ease. Your mother held your hand, tears streaking down her face like foregone stars plummeting from the sky. At the time, you found her reaction rash. Now, the reasons lined up like Dominos waiting for the fall.

"Why didn't she have an ..." You can't finish the sentence. It gets caught in your throat, a knotted lump that wouldn't recede.

Dad doesn't tell you he wanted her to have you. He doesn't say he didn't either. He continues to look at the cabinets, focusing with such force that he could have been counting the individual dust mites.

"We tried for a long time in between you and your sister to have another baby. We lost more than one."

You hadn't heard of these other babies. Hadn't seen any signs that your mother was capable or incapable of caring for anyone other than the two of you.

Once, before bedtime, your mother pulled you close against her. You had spent the day with your cousins and you were feeling bruised and burned by their scorn. When you were with them, you couldn't eat quickly enough or keep up with their continuous prattle. You didn't listen to the music they liked or read their books. You abhorred dolls. Your mother, who always smelled slightly of lavender, hugged you against her hips and got onto her knees. You remember thinking it took great effort to get to eye level.

"I'm the black sheep in this family," she said, nodding vigorously. "If I'm a black sheep, you're one too."

She kissed your nose then. You never asked her what she meant by that. Never weeded your way through the statement itself. But hearing that she fought for you, that she refused to let you go despite medical science, made you feel closer to her. Your dad said she cried as she held you that first time, fat ugly tears that contorted her face. He said she counted your fingers and toes aloud and kissed your eyelids and rubbed your thick hair under her nose to smell you. You wondered if she felt relief or ease or happiness. You wondered if you would've been a sheep if your eyes had looked different. If you weren't able to live an independent life. Before you can ask, your father reads your thoughts.

"She said when you were in her stomach that the two of you were simpatico. Soul mates."

*If I'm a sheep, you're a sheep,* she had said. You wish you had asked her more then, wished you had hugged her tighter and breathed in the smell of lavender blossoms that radiated from her. You wish you had asked her the perfume she wore. Now you go to the perfume counters in Macy's and Bloomingdale's and Nordstrom's looking for the scent that left glossy sunbursts on her neck following the spritz.

**Eight.** She wore a gold charm bracelet that jangled up and down her wrist as she spoke, when she turned the page in a book, as she yelled. This is cheating you suppose. You know that charm bracelet. Had you been blind folded and only able to identify her by touch, you would have grazed her right arm in search of it. But even now, in her death, as you wear the bracelet yourself, you didn't know where all the charms were from.

The heart was from an old boyfriend, his name long since forgotten. It's a little dented and misshapen. It looks like a deflated balloon. They didn't date long but it was long enough for him to love her. Your aunt said that came easily to her. Making people love her. She could wrap someone around her pinkie, seamlessly making them feel special and needed and desirable. She could look at you, her head tilted like an interested pelican, her eyes wide, and make you feel like you hung the moon.

The bundle of grapes is from California, a trip taken early in your parents' marriage. At a vineyard, your father refused to remove his shoes and socks. Mom didn't mind though. She slipped out of her loafers and allowed two porters to lift her into a barrel of grapes. She stomped vigorously and broke the skins beneath her feet as the juice stained her toes.

The pig was for her family farm. In the mornings, your mom would wake and feed the animals. She talked to them, her voice a high register as they ate the family's trash and muck. She never minded the dirt, letting it rest beneath her nails in straight black lines. Pigs were her favorite animals and sometimes, when she called you to dinner, she would do so with a spirited "shoo-eeeyyy," plopping platters on the kitchen table with gusto.

The ballet slippers were for her first dream. There are old black and white pictures, creased down the middle, that show your mother in tights and pointe shoes. Wide tutus circling her waist. Your Nana drove her to practices and recitals and watched her align her feet in varying positions. You can almost hear the notes, the music echoing through your mind. The patter of the soft sole shoes reverberating on wood floors. Your aunt said your mother didn't have much talent, though that didn't stop her from wishing, hoping, wanting. Needing something more than their little town in their little state that was rarely noticed for anything good.

The apple was from you and your sister, a gift you remember being remarkably proud of as a child when you saved money to buy your own Christmas gifts. You didn't know the various types of gold. Couldn't tell the difference between gold plated and 18K gold. You bought the plated. Now the apple looks rotten, decomposed from years of showers and swimming pools. It was an easy gift to identify her profession. Your mother was a teacher and now you can't think of anything she didn't teach you. Each time you cross the laces on your shoes, you think of her.

**Seven.** Her recipe for chocolate chip cookies was on the back of the Tollhouse package. You remember your mother baking a handful of delicious treats in the kitchen. Flour sifted through the air and had you licked the cabinet, it would've tasted like sugar. For her apple pies, she sliced apples so thin you could see the blade of the knife through the skin of the fruit. Her butterscotch cakes held tiny bulbs of butterscotch chips that were just the right texture. Her gallettis were perfectly fluffy waffles rich with honey. But her chocolate chip cookies were your favorite. Sometimes she would make them early in the morning, so early the smell woke you and you were left lying in bed wondering if it was a dream. The aroma pulled you through the house until you were standing in front of her, your hair a tangled weed matted from sleep. Sand-like crust solidified in the corner of your eyes. The two of you would sit with your backs warmed by the oven and gorge yourself on cookies until there were no cookies left when your sister and Dad came downstairs. There was only the lingering smell of chocolate pulsating through the kitchen.

Your mother allowed you to help bake the cookies. She tied an oversized apron around your neck and brought out a step stool from the closet for you to stand. Then, when you thought you had added all the ingredients. When the eggs had been cracked and the flour sifted and the chips stripped from the yellow bag, she would make you close your eyes. She would make you turn your back on the bowl and hum a little song. Now, you realize she must have been checking the recipe. She was likely reading through the list to make sure it was measured correctly, accurately, precisely. She always said, "Baking is a number's game. Cooking is about improvising." To distract you she would yank the spoon from the bowl, allowing you to run your tongue along its curved spine. She would tell you she was adding a little dash of love.

"I want to add love," you would say and she would laugh knowingly, a brazen laugh that filled every corner of the galley kitchen. A laugh that couldn't find a place to hide.

"You need big love for cookies Bug," she would say and you wondered if your love would ever be big enough, strong enough, loud enough to eclipse hers.

At the funeral, your sister made the cookies. You asked where she found the recipe and she laughed your mother's laugh. You closed your eyes and let it wash over you, feeling it warm your bones. It felt like salvation from a storm. A starving man's last meal. As you bit into them, you recognized the ingredients. You could pinpoint the amount of sugar, the quantity of vanilla extract. Still, something was missing. Something was forever lost.

**Six.** She was engaged when she met your father. You would've thought your dad would tell you this but he isn't one to rehash their love story. Your father is the man who showed his adoration by checking the pressure in your tires before a long trip. He couldn't say the word love aloud. It was her friend Mary who told you.

She was drinking an Arnold Palmer, sipping it casually through a florescent bendy straw. Her lipstick was smudged in a constellation against her front tooth, polka-dotted pink. She said it matter-of-factly, bluntly.

"Your mom was suppose to marry someone else."

You think of your parents. The way your father sat the style and obituary sections of the paper aside each morning so your mom could read them, the only portions she cared about. The way they shared cheater glasses, passing them back and forth in dark restaurants so they could both read the menu. Your father not caring that the specs were bright, aqua, cat-eye frames. The way your mother carried you to the kitchen, entertaining you with cartoons or baking or puppets while the Mountaineers were on. The sound of the announcers' voices coming through both the television and radio. Clashing into one another in a disruptive clatter that bothered you.

To you, your mom and dad were always halves of the same whole. You can't imagine a world where that wasn't the case.

"Your mom was always in love," Mary said. "She loved men in the Army and men in high school. She was a flirt. A tease."

She said it fondly, her mouth spread in a wide grin revealing those stained and crooked teeth.

"When a boy name Brian asked her to marry him, she said yes. I don't know if she ever thought she would go through with it."

You swish this other life around in your mind, allowing it to singe your brain.

"When did she meet Dad?"

Mary laughed again and you wished she wouldn't. Something felt urgent about this information, necessary.

"When she forgot to pay the phone bill on time. Your daddy was a lineman. She walked into the office and saw him. It was the day before Veterans' Day and he was wearing his Army uniform. He'd just come from a parade. Your mom got one glimpse of that man with his hair slicked to one side, that cowlick fluttering behind him, and she was done. His boss used to come in the office and know when Louise was there. She and your daddy would be in the back room."

You know other things about their life together so you wonder why this detail was omitted. You know that her father didn't come to the wedding, calling Daddy a WOP. You know they exchanged letters when your dad was in the reserves, letters he asked you to burn without reading upon his death. So, why not tell you about this other man she might have loved? You wondered if your mother was scared, fearful of what loving another man meant. Terrified of the life she missed or frightened of the one she almost missed?

**Five.** You mother cheated at card games. She cheated at board games. When you were seven, she taught you to play rummy. You were good at this game. You never told her but sometimes the cards you should play, those that needed to be discarded, would flash against your brain instinctually. If she was in a generous mood, she would have called this poppycock. If she was in a normal mood, she would have said bullshit. Her voice would've come out a croak, lower than other women as beautiful as your mother. You attribute the voice register to the years she spent smoking. As a toddler, tiny cigarette holes freckled your couch cushions and her clothes. When her father died in a fire, she quit cold turkey. Sometimes, though, she would buy cigarettes and smell the filters as you watched from the back seat of the car.

Your little family of four would play rummy on Friday nights in the fall. Your mother kept a spiral notebook, the cover torn in various places. Each week, your mom would write the date at the top of the page while your father built a fire in the stone fireplace. As you played, your mom would add the scores quickly in her head. She didn't always win. She lost often. Those weren't bad nights but they were awkward. You and your sister would go to bed early, your father pushing you through the motions of brushing your teeth. On nights when your mother won, she would put music on and the four of you would dance around your living room. She would hold your hand and twirl you around. She would put on bright red lipstick and kiss your cheeks so that your skin brandished her lips. You would go to bed rooting for her to win next week, her smell still lingering in your nose. Her voice echoing in your ears. Her lipstick plastered to your cheeks.

When you found the notebook, you hadn't thought much of it. You flipped through the pages and pages of numbers. They stopped abruptly and you realized the last date was just before you went to college. You read through the register and add the figures. The line at the bottom tells you it was a night your mother won, her name is circled in a bright red pencil. You still add though. You try to remember the night and realize with deep plunging sorrow that you can't. You wonder how many other nights with her you've forgotten. When you get to your score, you realize it's higher but your name isn't circled. You think this is petty of your mother and yet, you wish you had just let her win. You wish you had let her have a moment to dance with you and kiss you harder. You wonder how you felt at the time. You wonder if you ever begrudged her that but somewhere in her death, you've forgotten. Everything you remember is false, as if seen through fog.

**Four.** Your mother was forever afraid of disappointing her mother. Even after her death. Even after your Bubbie, as you called her, had been gone for years and all but permanently erased from your memory. Your aunt called her mother cold and withholding. You laughed when she said this, wondering how many years of therapy it had taken her to acquire that language. Your mother never said she was cold and withholding. She never said that she tried hard to be different. To raise you in a house where you laughed and danced and weren't afraid to tell her anything. Your aunt drank long slogs of a whiskey sour as you talked to her. When she went to the bathroom, you tasted the drink and grimaced, shocked by its strength and bitterness. When she came back, her lipstick reapplied and her scarf straightened, she poured the remainder of the drink down the drain. You looked around, anticipating cameras that revealed you'd stolen a sip. There weren't any.

"Why did Mom care if Bubbie was proud of her?"

You couldn't understand, couldn't fathom why her parenting mattered to anyone other than you and your sister. Maybe your father. But not to someone who was so decidedly different from her. You try to recall memories of your grandmother.

There's a photo hanging in your living room. In it, your grandmother and grandfather stare straight into the camera, your Bubbie's hair was a straight bob that brushed the undersides of her ears. Your mother is a baby and Bubbie is holding her, your mom's face obscured by the thin blanket. Your aunt was a little girl in a collared dress. She sat beside them. She had a dour expression sealed on her face. The picture is beautiful and sad. It reminds you of a Victorian painting.

You remember crying once, stretching your arms around Bubbie's knees while she filled a glass bottle with soda. Or … maybe you don't remember that exactly but instead recall the home video that revealed it. Still, it's clearly you and Bubbie in the frame. Your mother sat in the background at a round kitchen table smoking a cigarette while your sister snuggled in her lap. She was frowning and something within you understands now that she didn't want you to have the soda filled bottle. That it was against some rule of hers that you were only allowed to break at Bubbie's house.

You realize your aunt is talking and you haven't been concentrating. You were staring out the window, thinking.

"Your mother wanted her to agree with every decision she made until it came to your dad."

You realized then that your mother paid a price for her love. For your father. For the broken engagement. You realized that marrying a man who would provide and love you mattered little in a family with plenty of money. You're sad your mom was never sure-footed enough to step away from her mother entirely. You're disappointed there were so many unresolved issues lingering like washed laundry that didn't get the opportunity to dry.

**Three.** As you cleaned your parents' kitchen, you came across a cabinet with tens of hundreds of dishes. They were plain white with thin scallops around the edges. You had moved around that kitchen more times than you could count. Every holiday you all cooked together in a neat row. Each person had an assigned job. You made stuffed mushrooms, baking a line of caps in a mixture of olive oil and balsamic vinegar. Creating an interior combination of Italian sausage, garlic, sautéed onions, and cream cheese. Your sister sliced apples impossibly thin for dessert. Your father made sauce, continually stirring the crushed tomatoes with celery to sweeten the broth.

Your mom rolling homemade pasta dough into narrow strips, whipping the threads to braid them together. Your father's mother used to say your mother was too slow to make pasta. In a thick Italian accent, she would claim, "You a good girl Louise but you're so slow." Now you know you could never compete with her speed or her tidiness or the texture of her noodles.

You had been marking things for an estate sale. Purple stickers were things to keep for your father. Pink stickers were stuff you should take to your house. Yellow were ask your sister. Red were sale. The cabinet stuck a little as you pulled it open, wrenching your shoulder slightly in the process. You were tired and thin strands of hair got caught in the corner of your eyes.

"Daddy," you hollered as you glared at the dishes. Your eyes bulging with the realization that this was an unending project. The dishes didn't match but they were all similar. She had over twenty small condiment cups, things that would easily fit a hardboiled egg or tapenade or ketchup. Most likely ketchup.

Your dad had a slow shuffle, his speed even more sluggish without your mother's support. You sat on the floor with dust falling around you like snow flurries at the beginning of December. Your dad placed his hands on his knees, carefully dropping a pair of thick specs on the bridge of his nose. He touched the outline of a plate, running the pads of his fingers around the rims. You picked up one dish. It was stamped on the bottom. Benjamin's it said. Many of the dishes were from the restaurant that had recently shut down. The one where you ate every Mother's Day. The menus had been made to look like old-fashioned newspapers. The drinks were served in copper cups. Your mother always ordered the lamb chops with mint jelly. She would run the supple meat through the jam and suck aggressively on the shank. The mint was always served in the condiment cups and you realized your mother must have taken them. Slipping them into a purse or a to-go container. She had washed and rinsed and saved them long after the restaurant was gone. Long after she was gone.

**Two.** Your mother hated the smell of burnt toast. She hated the smell of burnt anything. You remember how she looked at your grandfather's funeral. She was wearing a navy polka dotted dress and four inch heels, a pearl necklace strung tightly against her collarbone. She was composed at first, at ease even, but that didn't stick. As you entered the wake, she paused, incapable of placing one foot in front of the other. She carried one of his handkerchiefs, the monogrammed 'A' standing out on white linen. It fluttered to the floor. It reminded you of the tutus you used to wear to ballet, the movement seamless and graceful and elegant.

Your grandfather died in a fire before either of them had the chance to say they were sorry. She hadn't spoken to him since she married your father. They said it was an electrical fire but everyone was a little skeptical, believing it could have been a smoldering cigarette nestled into the couch cushions. The casket is only open for the family and you wish it wasn't. You thought for a moment it might give you all closure but any solace is shucked from the room. It's replaced with desperation and cheap décor and empty sentiment.

Many people place things in the casket. You hadn't recognized that was something that's traditionally done but your mother puts in a small porcelain figurine and instructed you to write a thoughtful letter. You couldn't think of anything to say. You wrote the Lord's Prayer in neat cursive, signing your name at the bottom. You laid it next to your grandfather's shined, black dress shoes. You tried not to look at his face and hands, the only exposed areas of skin, but curiosity got the best of you and you ended up staring. He looked like a marshmallow left too long in the flames, the wrinkles in his face compressed and his skin dusty gray where the flames brushed it.

When it was your mother's turn, she tried to climb into the casket. She pushed and clawed and begged. Your father's strong forearms pulled her from the brink, his vein pulsing from the effort. She reared back and you thought she might spit in his face. Or slap him. It took an immense amount of effort to restrain her despite her size.

"He's burning," she said, clawing at your father's arm. "I can smell him dying."

You tried not to think your mother was crazy. Preferring despondent or in mourning. Still, you could only smell the industrial cleaner against the cheap funeral home carpeting. A hint of Pledge interrupted that. The spray used to bring the plastic plants to a high shine.

But your mother said it long after the funeral. During the campfire at Girl Scout Jamboree. When she carelessly burnt the meatloaf and once, when you tried to make her breakfast in bed and the toast was stiff with crusted black tendrils dangling from its underside.

Her stroke had surprised all of you. Your mother had previously been in good health, traveling and substitute teaching. Occasionally tutoring old students in French or geometry, subjects she was utterly ill-equipped to teach. You had been visiting her. The two of you sipping herbal tea laced with honey and talking about the latest book club book when her face slouched on one side. It looked like melted plastic. Her speech was slurred. You called your father and then an ambulance, later regretting the order of calls.

In the hospital, before your mother died of the stroke, your father was worried about the burnt toast. It was a rumor you'd heard from an old internet article. Or maybe from a book. You couldn't honestly remember. Your father paced in succinct circles, carefully placing one foot in front of the other. Your sister hadn't yet arrived.

"Mom hated the smell of anything burning," you said. Your father looked at you over his oversized square frames, his eyes drawn down in concern. You could tell he didn't know what you were talking about.

"I read somewhere that stroke victims smell burnt toast just before a stroke."

You hadn't heard from your sister or the doctors and your voice sounded intrusively loud in the hospital waiting room. You wondered if your father's mind would return to your grandfather's funeral the way yours had.

"That's a myth you know," an old woman leaned across the vinyl seats, resting her hands on its cracked arms. "I was a nurse for years. A couple of people have asked me about it since."

The woman had deep brown eyes that could be described as kind. It's the first time the description really fit.

"She hated the smell of burnt toast," your father said and for the first time you realized everyone does. You crossed your ankles and mouthed *thank you* to the retired nurse. You wanted to ask her other things. What was the probability of your mother's survival? What was the recovery time? Could you still talk to her, bundled under a pile of quilts, as you watched bad television? You didn't though.

You breathed in deeply, releasing the air through your puckered lips. You thought you smelled burned toast and wished for a rupture in your brain to take you, to drag you under and carry you to your mother.

**One.** Your mother left once before this. You were an infant and your sister was a toddler. You don't remember her being gone and you struggled momentarily to reckon it with the woman you knew. The one you now know.

Your sister can't remember this, despite being nearly four.

Your father doesn't mention it. You wonder if he could or if his brain erased it to prevent pain.

It wasn't Mary either. Though, when you mentioned it to Mary, she blushed crimson and avoided direct eye contact.

You found a shoe box. It was upside down in the far corner of her closet. You shook it hard, realized momentarily the contents were sparse. You slid to the floor, the crown of your head rested against the wall and your eyes slammed shut. You wanted this task, the endless packing, to be over but you knew, once it was, another piece of your mother will be gone. You opened the lid slowly, skipping it across the floor. There are a handful of postcards in the box. Each is dated from September to November 1970. One features a dark night, the Golden Gate bridge scorched against the sky. Another has a Statue of Liberty, her green frame imposing. A Chicago skyline, the Space Needle, the Washington Monument. Five words are written on the back of each postcard. *Dear Girls, I can explain …*

No explanation followed and you realized there isn't one. There can't be an explanation succinctly written on a postcard to rationalize deserting your babies.

You thought of your daughter. The way she worried when you got home late from work. The way she watched you fold laundry. When she rested her head against your breastbone, falling easily into a dreamless sleep. You can't imagine a day without her but that's too simple. It's like remembering your mother. It's too easy to fixate on the good without digging through the beautiful chaos of the everyday.

You wondered if the list you've assembled brought you any closer to her. Did that even matter? She's gone now. You were abandoned and deserted and alone. You held the postcards in your hands, shuffled them over and over.

"Explain," you said into the ether of the room. "Why did you leave?"

You don't know if you mean then or now. You listened closely for an answer and when none came, you pocketed the postcards, unwilling to suffocate them in the bottom of the white trash bag.

You finally found an answer.

Proof that your mother was a person rather than a figment of your imagination.

She lived and breathed and baked and cheated and hated and loved and left, once by choice.

Once without warning.

You touched your chest, massaging your heart as you realized once and for all that she's gone.

# *Incompetent*

THE sky was bruised purple the day Caro and Bill set out to scatter the ashes of their stillborn son. Caro stared at the clouds from the vanity in her childhood bedroom. She lightly rubbed her chest, trying to massage the bowtie of anxiety that formed there as she memorized the cloud's exact hue. To Caro, the baby felt West Virginian. She wanted to give him roots in the rich mountain soil. Selfishly, she also needed a resting place where she would always return.

Caro slowly laced up a pair of tan hiking boots, allowing the supple leather tops to cut into her calves. The mirror on the wall highlighted her swollen face, one she didn't recognize. Her cheeks were round and full. The cheeks of a chubby newborn. Her hair hung in distressed strands. At the beginning of each pregnancy it would thicken, coming in full and rich. Then, as her body turned against her it would fall out in heavy clumps that stopped the drain.

Bill, her husband, dressed beside her, his back curved as he slipped a thick pair of jeans over his hips. Bill's smooth skin and full head of ash blond hair were unfazed despite the death of their child. Despite the two miscarriages prior.

Caro slid a bellyband around her waist, the rolls of fat above her uterus preventing her from buttoning the top button. She smoothed the stray wisps of hair into a ponytail and, lifting her shirt, strummed the lines that stained her stomach like coffee spilled down a Carrera countertop. Bill patted her forearm, rubbing an intersection of blue-green veins.

"Ready?" he asked.

Bill looked strong and confident. He was willing to move forward, one foot in front of the other. Caro begrudged that but she nodded solemnly, happy to follow his lead.

Caro's mother was sitting on the porch, her white hair twisted into a low bun. She held thick needles that manipulated yarn in what Caro assumed was a baby blanket. Her mother had knitted two others, giving them away following each loss. This one was nearly completed with triangular rows of alternating blue and cream stitches. Bill carried a small shoebox, their child's cremated body. Caro's arms were noticeably empty. Her mother stood, wrapping Caro in an awkward hug.

"God takes care of his children," she said.

Caro tried not to roll her eyes. She pivoted, facing her house. Every time she came home, it felt a little smaller, more compact. She wondered if she was Alice in Wonderland. If she had swallowed a vial of potion that made her too big, too fast. The paint on the clapboard siding was chipped and weathered.

The floorboards on the porch groaned under her weight. Four beautiful quarter horses stood in the pasture to her right, a dilapidated fence made of warped wood kept them from running away. A few friendly waddling ducklings nearly got squished under their hooves.

"Should I come with you all?" her mother asked.

"Maybe it should just be us," Caro said. Some part of her wanted to do it alone. Another didn't want to scatter the ashes at all. A light rain started, tip-tapping against the tin roof. The rain smell musky, like the earth. Her mother repositioned herself in the rocking chair, the knitting needles clapping together in a steady one-two rhythm.

"It's raining," Bill said, staring hard at the sky as he stated the obvious.

"I think it should be raining," Caro said.

Caro thought of the day her son was born, the day he died. The sun had broken through the blinds, an intrusive beam shaking her awake. Just as she was starting to enjoy the view, Caro was stunned by a cramp. It was a feeling remnant of her period. Her back and hips and rib cage and chest bunched and throbbed. Blood slipped through her underwear, a steady line of red. The bed was wet with her blood and sweat and Bill woke, disgusted. His hands were coated in liquid and the acrylic smell of the baby dying attacked both of them.

"Jesus," Bill said, rolling to the edge of the bed, away from the mess. "Jesus, Caro. Get up. Go to the bathroom. Something's wrong." His voice sounded both manic and abrasive. It broke through the pain, startling her.

Caro didn't move. For a while, she just lay in the mess until she felt light-headed while Bill consulted the Internet, the baby books. Then, she stood and slowly shuffled to the bathroom, unsteady and shaking and barely able to lift her feet. She heard Bill call the doctor.

"Should we come immediately?" Bill asked. Caro listened to him pace a succinct circle around the bedroom as she rested on the bathroom tiles. She couldn't crawl into the fetal position, the baby bump blocking the path. She wanted to though. Moments like this were fetal position worthy.

Bill came into the bathroom without knocking. She could see that he had stripped their bed. He spooned Caro, pressing a firm palm on her temple.

"His name was Jack," she told him as he gawked at her shattered frame. "I know we hadn't talked about it, but that's what I wanted to call him."

Caro felt an urgent need to push. A leaden weight pressuring her abdomen. More blood came out and Caro instinctively sensed her child wasn't far behind. His weight bore down on her rectum and she had to calm herself, practicing the breathing from birth class, so that the message was clear. No baby, no real baby, would be the aftereffect of the pain.

"I like that name," Bill said.

Caro wanted to scream and cry. She wanted to rip her skin from the bone and walk around as a collective of muscles and bones and blood and organs and cells. Anything but herself.

"Want me to call your mom?" Bill offered. He sat too close to her, breathing her air. A sense of claustrophobia attacked her.

"No," Caro replied, unwilling in that moment to pray.

The doctor didn't call it a miscarriage. He called it *fetal demise* due to an *incompetent cervix*. The baby died tangled and trapped and choked within Caro's womb. In the hospital, they inserted a twelve-inch needle into Caro's spine. Iciness flowed through her veins, and the cramps became an uncomfortable tingle against her abdomen. The doctors told her when to push. The delivery took longer because the baby couldn't help, couldn't wriggle and worm his way out. Bill waited outside. Caro arched her back slightly. The nurse counted to ten each time she pushed, her voice a sweet whisper into the bone behind Caro's ear. When they lifted the child from her, there was no scream. The cord was wrapped so tightly around his throat that he was light purple. His ears were tiny conch shells and his lips were plump and full. Bill came in and Caro handed the doctor her cell phone.

"Do you mind?" she asked, her throat sore from the medication and outright exhaustion.

The doctor washed his hands thoroughly, soaping his forearms. He took a picture of the three of them, one of the first Caro had been in where someone didn't instruct her to smile or say cheese.

In the days following, Caro thought of nothing but her dead son. She fixated on Jack as she was Cloroxing the sheets. When she mopped the floor. She took showers, long and scalding baths, where she scrubbed every inch of herself but she still didn't feel clean. She prayed. She just wanted the pain to be surgically removed.

Now, Caro regretted all those prayers whispered hastily in hushed tones. She lamented her lack of faith as she cursed God for the damage he inflicted. She was resentful of her mother's belief. Of Bill's composure. Of every woman capable of maintaining a pregnancy.

Midway up the mountain Caro and Bill saw two deer, a doe and fawn, their tawny fur flecked with white, eating peacefully from a cluster of wild blackberries. The fawn licked her lips and swayed beside her mother. When the deer heard Caro and Bill's footsteps stomping the leaves underfoot, the doe nudged the fawn forward. Ever-weary of humans.

Caro pulled Bill off the trail and they walked through the brush until they reached an old maple with a U-shaped branch. Caro used to sit in it as a child. Her initials were carved into the base. She hauled herself onto the seat that overlooked the mountain. The rain had nearly stopped, but water still slid down the peaks, turning dust to mud. The animals were starting to make noises around her, shuffling from their hiding places. Caro whispered her son's name again. Imagined him sitting next to her in this place that she loved and deplored with equal veracity.

"What do you think he would have been like?" She asked. "Do you think he would have played baseball?"

"I like to think he would have been a little like you. Nose in a book. Somewhat afraid of the dark. A snuggler." Bill inched closer to Caro, the box a fixture on his hip. "With some of me thrown in," he said, letting out a nervous laugh. "Maybe he'd love dinosaurs and know how to make truck noises with his mouth."

Bill held his hand out and Caro climbed down from the tree. She was restless and scraped the dirt from the forest floor. All signs of the rain were gone except for the dew on the leaves and the mud.

"How do you love something that isn't real?" Caro asked.

The mountains swallowed her question. She bent and picked a few dandelions. They were weeds but she'd always loved them. She rubbed the flower on Bill's forearm until it stained his skin. Then she marked herself in the same place. Partners. Handcuffed in grief. She led him further into the woods.

Finally, towards the top of the trail, Caro and Bill veered left into their favorite spot. She had taken him here when they were first dating, long before Jack or the other babies. Back when hope radiated easily from them, the gift of youth.

A wide valley stretched before them with a few errant lavender plants and an old twisting oak in one corner. The tall stalks made a loud swish against her thick jeans, leaving a streak of purple fuzz. Caro took Bill's hand, lacing their fingers together in a firm grasp. She walked to the center of the field and laid down. Caro longed for more of the black magic that was parenthood. She wished she had kissed the seashell ears. She wished Bill had gotten to know the way their child loved the sun, moving against Caro's hand in the morning heat.

Caro rested her hands against her stomach now and allowed the breath to fill her lungs. She smelled the mud. She felt desperately lost, constipated with fear for all the things her life hadn't brought. She conjured the image of Jack, pondering what the other babies who'd died inside her looked like. She wiped the dirt from her hands and signaled for Bill to follow. They walked to the oak.

"Here," she said to Bill. He slowly pried the lid from the box and gently shook the ashes onto the ground. Caro took a handful. She ground her son's remains into her palms, tattooing everything she touched with Jack.

"I love you," she said. She kissed her own hand as if it was her son's head. It was her last act of motherhood. Her unconditional, unwavering, unfiltered love.

# The Special One

THE father and his grown daughter stand in the kitchen, their hands slick from egg whites and grainy from parmesan. They have been trying all day to recreate the recipe, and their discarded efforts are littered across the marble counters, seeping into the porous stone. The oil bubbles, occasionally popping with a menacing growl that makes the girl slide into the cool hug of the stainless steel refrigerator.

With each new attempt, the daughter preps the cauliflower the same way, rinsing the pale head carefully until it appears whiter in the abrasive kitchen light. Her father cleaves off chunks before they batter them in varying combinations of eggs, parsley, salt, parmesan. When her father drops the vegetable into the oil, the heavy smell lingers, suctioning to the walls. It's animalistic, pure. The popping grease flies like shrapnel, so the father stands over the daughter's right shoulder, a safe distance from the debris. He watches her turn the fried pieces with a fork, her arms a red landmine of burns.

The recipe was one his mother made. Now they can't remember the process. The father has asked the daughter to try. *Please think*, he says. *Please help*. The daughter only remembers her grandmother teaching her to grate cheese, demonstrating how to roll her fingers back from the metal grates as they separated cheese from rind.

Her father rarely asks her to do anything so she agreed. Now, in the room full of spoiled food and dashed expectations, she regrets this compliance. She could be home with her daughter. They could be finger painting or planting flowers.

*This is the one*, her father says, as he slips the freshly fried cauliflower bits onto a paper towel and pats them dry. They haven't spoken much this afternoon so, her silence is irrelevant. She scoops the remaining half of the breaded cauliflower with a fork, sliding it from the oil like a woman slithering from a steamy bath. The father gazes eagerly at his portion. For a moment, the daughter feels better about being here. She pushes aside the thought that he persistently and vocally wishes she were someone else:

As tidy and feminine as her mother.

As smart as her brother was allowed to be.

As demure and kind as her own daughter.

She shoves her old resentments deep into her stomach—things she wishes he'd say, like how proud he is of her—because she hopes this experience will be a special one. That they'll reincarnate a piece of her grandmother.

The father takes a bite, his teeth severing the cauliflower's neck. He gargles it in his mouth before savagely spitting it into a napkin.

*It's not hers*, he says. Once again, the daughter deflates. She is only herself. Only that. Always capable of being who she is without ever truly being who he wants.

## Peanuts and Rubies

THE tidiness in the hospital reminded Ruth of her son Tom. As a child, Tom had collected acorns from the yard—making a basket from the folds of his t-shirt. He baked the hollowed out casings on a low brick retaining wall that separated their house from the neighbor's. The rows of oak shells were perfect lines in structured patterns. Twenty shells snuggled against jagged bricks like bodies sunning themselves against smooth, beige sand. Tom counted them slowly, the soft pad of his pointer finger bopping the acorn carcasses without shuffling the design. Everything in the NICU had that level of precision. The buttons on the heart rate machine looked like Tom's grid. The rectangle tiles behind the nurse's station were stacked in horizontal rows. Even the supply closet, with its columns of boxed latex gloves brought Ruth back to those tiny tiers of random organization.

Ruth pushed a stubborn cart filled with plush brown teddy bears and vibrant balloons to assigned glass cubicles. The spaces were small and translucent, and Ruth thought the intrusiveness—the ability to see every moment of suffering and strength, miracles and misfortune—was the worst part. Ruth wondered if the parents played the numbers game like she did. Do their ears perk up when the heart rate monitors blare through the narrow halls? Its long consistent wail the signal of death. Do they count the patients in the cubes? Calculate how many need to die statistically for their child to live?

Ruth was a retired accountant and numbers were always her friends. There was a comfortable certainty in digits—until Tom's diagnosis. Ruth let the figures play on an endless loop in her mind. The stats came from trifold pamphlets and late night Internet searches, her fingers smashing the buttons with loud clacks. She consumed the information like PAC-MAN gnawing through dotted swatches.

*ALS patients typically survive two to five years post diagnosis.*
*Twenty percent live longer than five years.*
*One hundred percent of ALS patients die from the disease.*

Tom hadn't reached a year yet but already the tremor in his hands compromised his ability to drive. He couldn't tie a knot in his shoelaces. Couldn't sign a check with his normal slanted scrawl—handwriting that was messy and typical of a lefty.

The wheels of the cart rotated abruptly nearly veering into the wall. Ruth redirected, backing it up to avoid the crash. She rearranged the teddy bears, remembering Tom's snuggy, the old Snoopy that was worn and bald on the stomach. Ruth had seen the stuffed animal recently. It still smelled like Tom, like freshly cut grass, cedar, and gnawed-on strawberries.

She wondered if it was better to have the memories? She thought about the nights when she made Tom and her younger son, Ben's, favorite meal—homemade mac and cheese rich with nutmeg and sharp cheddar. Could she make that again without seeing Tom's wide grin, all teeth and dimples, at the end of their scratched kitchen table? Could she watch the Cubs without imagining Tom's second grade cowlick bobbing along the third base line in a blue and white striped jersey smeared with mud? Could she read Gatsby without picturing the shadow box scene Tom had created in ninth grade? Was it better to be robbed from the years up front? Cheated from the childhood or tortured by the everyday triggers?

Ruth kept her head down, trying to avoid eye contact with the mothers who rubbed the bridge of their baby's noses through the holes cut in the incubator sides. She didn't want to talk for fear of what she'd reveal. Didn't want to blurt the simple truth. That she couldn't waste her prayers for a miracle on them when she needed one for herself.

By one, Ruth was ready to leave. She saw her husband, Sherm, step from the elevator onto her floor, shuffling his feet in battered boat shoes, hands in his pockets. His blue beach cap, streaked white from the sun and the salt of the ocean, was pulled low over his eyes.

Normally, she and Sherm met by the nursery. Ruth would find him crying in front of the wall of babies—each wrapped in a white scratchy blanket, a pink and blue striped hat situated low over their foreheads and ears. So new. So fresh. Sometimes his tears were slow and meticulous, other times gushing sobs that racked his chest. Part of her loved him for it and she would extend her hand, now lined with green veins and skin that rippled from the bone. He would hold it for a minute then shove both their hands into the pocket of his windbreaker.

Other times, Ruth resented his tears. They were bitter bites of salt water that couldn't alter or alleviate anything. Ruth didn't cry often, even after Tom's diagnosis. So she begrudged the frequency of Sherm's emotion. It was a banner he carried, a sandwich board that communicated his pain and his evolution and his journey as a parent. Ruth read once that a majority of families who suffer the loss of a child disintegrate. Ruth shook her head in an attempt to remove the visceral image of her alone from her mind. The action reminded her of the Etch-A-Sketch Tom and Ben used to play with. They moved it up and down in frustrated spurts to erase the picture.

Ruth swallowed loudly and squeezed Sherm's long rope-like fingers. Today, perhaps because Sherm hadn't made it to the babies, there were no tears.

Ruth exhaled in relief.

"I'll get my things," she said, satisfied with the mitzvah for the day. Tom was coming to dinner tonight and she allowed the excitement to flush through her chest and cheeks. She wanted to boil potatoes, bake apple kugel, soak the brisket, and heat the challah.

"I'll come with you," Sherm said without pause.

Ruth opened a heavy door to the volunteer lounge. She pulled her purple raincoat over her slumped shoulders. As they were walking to the elevator, Ruth saw Father Marcus transitioning from one cube to the next. Father Marcus was her favorite priest at Northwestern Hospital. His skin was tanned leather with deep pocket marks. His collar always looked a little too tight under the strain of a bulging neck. His pants, two inches too short, showcased white athletic socks, but his laugh was calming—a bubbly giggle that rose from his throat like freshly popped champagne. He remembered all the volunteers' names, and when Tom was diagnosed, Father Marcus had his parish whisper prayers. Ruth received casseroles and cards and too many copies of *The Year of Magical Thinking* from his congregation. And yet, he still had prayers for the babies. Ruth despised her own selfishness.

"What do you say, when you pray over the children?" Ruth had asked him once, her curiosity piqued when she was in the early days of Tom's diagnosis. When she couldn't sleep and all food tasted like sawdust.

"I pray the prayer of Saint Gerard."

Ruth had never heard of Saint Gerard. She didn't want to tell Father Marcus that, embarrassed by her ignorance. Ruth adjusted her hand-knit scarf, feeling itchy within her own skin.

"I could say it now," Father Marcus said.

His hand firmly gripped Ruth's before she could protest, and she tried not to focus on her clammy palms, the consistency of raw scallops. Father Marcus bowed his head and Ruth noticed the thinning against his scalp. She stared at a spot on the wall, a large divot in the drywall most likely caused by the repetitive banging of wheelchairs.

"We thank God for the great gift of our son and ask him to restore our child to health if such is His holy will. This favor, we beg of you through your love for all children and mothers. Amen."

Father Marcus opened his eyes, but Ruth was somewhere else. She was swimming through Tom's childhood, their life with him.

Now, seeing Father Marcus made her uncomfortable. He was a reminder of the palpable guilt she couldn't escape.

"There's your friend," Sherm said. Without giving Ruth time to respond,

Sherm headed in the direction of Father Marcus. The two men shook hands and Ruth marveled at how small Sherm looked in the shadow of the priest's statuesque frame. She approached them slowly, carefully placing one foot in front of the other as if she were walking on a balance beam.

"Tom's coming this evening," Ruth heard Sherm say in a loud whisper. Soon she was next to the men, and the three formed a strange huddle.

"He'll take the train?" Father Marcus asked. Ruth wondered if the question was mere curiosity or a clever attempt to discern Tom's physical state. Sherm nodded.

"I hope he's doing well," Father Marcus said. "I should continue."

Ruth watched as he walked into another room without trepidation. The mother, a young girl who might be twenty, looked so scared. Her eyes were swollen from a lack of sleep. Her stomach still had a pooch from the recent delivery. Her nails were pointed cat claws painted bright pink. The two stood beside the incubator that looked like the glass casket from *Snow White*. Father Marcus held his hands over the crib, talked to the girl for a moment, then began his prayer. An older lady pushed past Ruth as Father Marcus and the girl bowed their heads over an infant boy with black curls and a round face. The lady nearly knocked Ruth over.

"Get away from him," the older lady, possibly the grandmother, shouted. "That baby doesn't need last rites or whatever you're performing."

The two women faced one another as if in a Western duel. Ruth couldn't look away. The girl straightened her cotton pajamas and shoved a stalk of shocking red hair behind one ear.

"It's a prayer. He's just offering a prayer," she said, her voice soft at first then crescendoing with her agitation.

"We don't need pity. He doesn't need more prayers," the older woman said.

Father Marcus retreated from the room, his palms up in a surrender's stance. Ruth hadn't noticed the small black diaper bag until the girl picked it up harshly, spilling some of the contents onto the floor. She threw it hard with a grunt. The bag sailed towards Ruth, narrowly missing her head, then landing with a soft thud against the stained tile floor. Tiny diapers and wipes, a pacifier and a sealed bottle of formula clattered from it during the decent.

"I want every prayer," the girl yelled. "He needs all of them."

The girl stood before the crib, pressed her hands against the transparent sides to shield the baby's light eyes. Ruth watched the scene as if it were a soap opera. Sherm grabbed her arm, his fingers biting into her fleshy bicep, and led her towards the exit. She tripped over her feet and would have fallen had it not been for Sherm's firm grip.

In the elevator, Ruth felt winded, and a torrent of tears slipped in jagged lines down her face, catching in the wrinkles by her neck. Once the first was released, she couldn't stop them. She bent forward, resting her hands on her knees. She cried with the unstoppable force of someone retching on all fours.

"She's me," Ruth said, recognizing the level of pain and outrage and indignation within the girl. Realizing the shitty hand they both had been dealt. "I want all of them," Ruth repeated the girl's words to herself through sobs.

On the drive home, Ruth pressed her hand against the window to feel the cold. She wanted it to penetrate her skin and course through her limbs with its chill. It reminded her that she could feel something other than pain or fear. She was still here and Sherm was still here and Tom was still here. Ruth could still touch his face, hear his laugh at the end of a familiar story. She could still be angry with him, resentful that he'd been sick and sought help without her. "I want them all," Ruth said again to herself, knowing it was the truth. Accepting that all the prayers wouldn't help.

Despite cooking brisket for over forty years, the meat was dry. Ruth, Sherm, and Tom chewed in monotonous silence. Since this afternoon, Ruth kept replaying the incident with the girl. Her hair the color of an afternoon sunset the night before a storm. Her words and tone—the venom laced with crumbling expectations—rang in Ruth's ears.

Tom looked exhausted, deep crescent moons beneath his eyes. Hollow cheeks further accentuated his high cheekbones. Ruth thought the thinness in Tom's face made him haggard. His watch scaled his arms, no longer tethered by a strong wrist. The meat wavered at the end of his fork as he ate. Ruth resisted the urge to spoon-feed him as she had when he initially tried sweet potatoes as a baby.

"Are you eating?" Ruth asked. She had a million other questions but fought her natural instinct, the one that told her to bombard Tom with inquiries.

"Yep," Tom muttered, the response of a sullen teenage rather than a man towards the end of his life.

The television droned in the other room, spouting commentary about a recent robbery in Wicker Park. The story further depressed Ruth. She stacked the dishes, an old English patterned china that once belonged to her mother. On its border, blue women carried an assortment of jars, shouldering the type of burdens women have for ages. Most of the plates were chipped around the edges.

Sherm popped the tops from two beers, handing one to Tom. Then, he mixed a vodka tonic with three lime wedges, the same drink Ruth had drunk every evening since 1972. Ruth left the tower of plates soaking in the sink. They all retired to the living room, sitting in the same spots they always sat in. Tom in the angle of an L-shaped couch. Ruth in a tall wingback covered in a fabric that featured frolicking lions. Sherm in a beat-up leather chair, worn on the arms and stained with water rings.

"How's work?" Sherm asked.

Tom was a special ed teacher at a South Side elementary school.

In any other family, the question was typical. In their home, it was tangled with medical baggage. The doctors had advised Tom not to work. To sleep often. To limit movement. To live with his parents. Ruth had sat quietly through the appointment, trying to ignore the loud clang of a wall clock. Tom had simmered beside her, anger and injustice radiating from him as the doctor's methodical voice spelled out Tom's abbreviated life.

"An invalid," Tom had said with a scoff.

He spit the word out like it was a rotten tomato. The doctor made a tent with his hands. Ruth brushed Tom's forearm. She wanted to restrain his anger but she inflamed it instead.

"Don't piss on my head and call it rain," Tom said, standing clumsily after a noticeable stumble. "No one knows what accelerates this."

Now, in her own home, Ruth wiped the condensation from her glass and watched her son closely. The lime juice in her drink smelled crisp, like relaxation.

"My class is small this year and I have an aide," Tom said. "I'm tired at the end of the day. Sometimes I walk into the apartment and get in bed with all my clothes on."

"Do the kids know?" Sherm asked.

"Nah," Tom said, waving a shaking hand and raising the beer to his lips. It rattled against his bottom teeth. "The kids wouldn't really understand. A few of them are high functioning, but they still wouldn't get it."

The three of them stared at the television for a moment, and Ruth was unsure how to direct the conversation.

"I want to talk to you guys about something before I leave," Tom said.

He wiped his hands on his pants and treaded to the other room, his feet landing with a thud against the hard wood floors. He retrieved a manila envelope from his frayed canvas satchel. He flopped back down with a clumsy thud. There were flyers and pamphlets sticking from the end of the file. The only one Ruth could see was for Graceland Cemetery. He spread them in a careful fan across the oak coffee table. Ruth tried to focus on the papers and not the scratches in the wood's surface. She ran her red acrylic nail through one elongated divot, distracting herself.

"I've made plans," Tom said. "So you don't have to."

He poked at the paperwork, his finger landing too hard and shaking the surface. The papers were varied but Ruth could see information about the cemetery, coffins, a written obituary that was only five lines, a will that was about the same length, three letters addressed to Ruth, Sherm, and Ben. At the edge of the table was a brochure with bright red letters. Kailua-Kona Legacy Program, The 38th Annual Ironman, it read. Ruth pulled it from the pile.

"What's this?" she asked.

"I wanted to talk about it last," Tom said.

"I understand everything else. Leave it, we'll keep it all in the security deposit box," Ruth said quickly. "But what's this?"

"It's something I'm going to do, Mom. It the last thing I want."

Tom pointed to the obituary.

"If I can't do it, if my body quits, then take out the last line of the obit."

"I'm confused, Tommy," Ruth said, reverting to the name they'd called him as a child. "What is this?" She enunciated each word carefully, allowing her tongue to rest on the roof of her mouth.

"Last week, I entered the lottery for the Iron Man in Hawaii, Mom," Tom began. "They literally pull names from a hat if you can't qualify. If my name is chosen, then I'm going to compete. I'm going to finish."

"That's a hell of a challenge," Sherm said. "Even for the healthiest participant." His voice sounded too loud. It bounced off the walls and the eight-foot ceiling. Ruth felt as if they were discussing a book she hadn't read.

"Yeah," Tom said. He exuded confidence and Ruth wondered how that was possible in his condition.

"It's a race?" Ruth asked. Tom and Sherm nodded in unison.

"It's a triathlon," Tom said. "A 2.4-mile swim, one hundred and twelve miles on the bike, then you run a 26-mile marathon."

"Almost one hundred and forty one miles in your condition," Ruth said, doing the math quickly.

"Yeah," Tom replied. If he said "yeah" one more time, Ruth thought she might choke him. She thought about the adolescent years when she would've longed for this sort of quiet nonchalance, but Tom had been loud then. He'd listened to grunge, worn dirty clothes torn at the knees, littered their car with Sex Pistols cassettes and cigarette buds that Ruth tried hard to ignore.

"How will you train? You aren't even supposed to walk often," she said, her voice barely a whisper. Ruth gulped her drink. She thought again of the mother this morning. She wished she could bury her expectations and her anger instead of her son. She tried not to yell and failed.

"You can't possibly do this," Ruth said. "It will cut what's left of your life in half."

Tom doubled over with laughter, propping his head up with his hands. Ruth thought again of the son she used to know. Tom riding a blue two-wheel bike with a bell at Kinder Care. Spitting on skinned knees and bruised elbows to show his bravado. To prove that nothing could hurt him.

"That's the life the doctors want me to live, that you want me to live. It's nothingness. Nothing to look forward to other than dying. Nothing to hope for, to strive for."

Ruth folded and unfolded the pamphlet.

"I was at the NICU this morning and there was this mother. She was so mad but when I looked closely, she was terrified," Ruth said.

She concentrated on her palms. A psychic at a college sorority party once told her she'd live a long happy life. That she'd have two sons and a few grandkids, and they would be close. Ruth suddenly wanted a refund. She felt gypped, cheated from a good life because of this blemish.

Tom stood and collected the papers. He shoved them in the folder and sat on the coffee table.

"I need you, Mom."

Ruth reached for Tom's hand. She noticed how young he felt, his skin buoyant and smooth. His hair full.

"I need this," he whispered. Ruth wondered if Sherm heard, if he was still there. Her eyes were closed so tightly that she was beginning to see gray dots. Then, she felt Sherm beside her too, his hands roughly massaging a knot from her shoulders.

"Ruth, remember the story the rabbi told at our wedding?" Sherm said. His voice startled her.

"What story?" Tom asked.

"The peanuts and the rubies. I thought it was glib at the time," he said.

Ruth hadn't thought of it in a long time. Sometimes, she still felt as young as she had that day when her skin was smooth and taut, an ivory dress pooling at her feet. She remembered the silky texture of the shawl that was draped over her slim pale shoulders. The same shawl that would be repurposed as Tom's baby blanket. Ruth's family beneath the chuppah looked scared and excited. She knew nothing. She had lived in the same house, in the same town where she was born. She had known Sherm since elementary school, loved him since high school. He was a man who read poetry and listened to Etta James songs in the car. The man who retold their son a story from their wedding.

"There was a man and a woman," Sherm began. "In the beginning of their marriage they were very poor but on their first anniversary, the husband wanted to get his wife something. He bought her a brown paper bag filled with peanuts. Years passed and the family became prosperous. The wife grew ill though. Lung cancer. On their fortieth anniversary, the man wanted to buy his wife something. He brought home a brown paper bag filled with rubies." Sherm stopped. Tom's hand trembled lightly, an unstoppable jitter. His eyes shifted from his mother to his father and back.

"The wife said, 'I wish more than anything it were filled with peanuts,'" Ruth said.

"You don't appreciate anything at the time it's happening," Sherm said. "Not when they're little and only want to sit in your lap. Then, all you want is space."

"Or when they have a bad dream and curl into the crook of your arms. I swear some mornings I didn't even know how you boys had gotten there," Ruth said. She smoothed Tom's hair from his forehead and resisted the urge to tell him she needed him, too. Tom sucked in the air, his breathe rasping in his chest.

She turned the pamphlet over and over in her hands, smoothing the glossy page.

"I don't know if my name will be chosen, Mom," Tom said. "I don't know anything. But I signed up for the lottery last week."

Tom leaned forward and lightly rubbed Ruth's arms.

"I need something to look forward to."

"At least we got the peanuts," Ruth said.

Ruth stared at Tom's face and noticed the way a single freckle peeked through the stubble. She took in the exact color of his bright eyes. She memorized the way his voice sounded. The way his fingers were so long they bent slightly to the right. The way he smelled like cedar and how his left hand always had pencil smudges along it. All she wanted were peanuts.

Ruth thought again of the young mother in the hospital and she silently extended that prayer to her.

# A Piece of Me

NETA carried two boxes into every new apartment and throughout each fresh relationship. One of the boxes was tangible, made of cardboard, and molding in the corners. The other was an emotional black box stored somewhere between her conscious and subconscious. Each time she traveled further from her past, she pulled her collections down and examined the sparse contents of her childhood.

Nestled against the cardboard were three black seashells with pink underbellies. The ocean had eaten holes in them but they were otherwise intact. A Roald Dahl book stolen from the Madison Public Library whose pages were worn thin and bent at the corners, the poor man's bookmark. A blue ribbon her sisters, Lottie and Isabell, used to tie in her hair to keep unruly wisps from her eyes. A key to the first car she'd ever owned, a 1996 maroon Ford Taurus with mismatched hubcaps that her grandfather bought from a dying neighbor. A picture of her and her oldest sibling Henry on the shoreline at Kitty Hawk. She was tiny, 6 or 7, wearing a red suit that was two sizes too big and Henry looked out of place with his blue jeans rolled up, the ocean licking his naked feet. And a plastic baggie, coated in white powder.

It wasn't until she got to the baggie that she unpacked the second box. The heavier one. The one which ensured sleepless nights and endless therapy. The baggie was what stole her mother, long before Neta had an opportunity to know her. Sometimes she opened it and slipped her nose between the folds. She wasn't sure what oxy smelled like and yet she could remember the texture of it beneath her fingers. She couldn't remember the tenor of her mother's voice when she was happy but could perfectly envision the way she hovered above the powder, inhaled quickly, and sat back against the couch with satisfaction. Had someone fingerprinted the bag, they would've found prints of everyone in Neta's household. Everyone who enabled her. But Neta imagined only her mother touching this bag. She imagined her hands where Neta's were. Her thumbs sealing the contents.

Neta had no desire to be like her mother. And yet, there was comfort in holding something she held. There was no acceptance. No forgiveness. And yet, as much as she didn't want to admit it, somewhere in the well of Neta's soul, love remained.

Whenever these sentimental moments overcame her, Neta would conjure a picture of her mother at her worst. Skinny, strung out. Her hair hanging in matted tendrils. Her arms skeletal, unable to provide cushion or warmth. She would recall her mother spanking her sister Lottie with a wooden spoon for buying too many groceries, as if their hollow, distended stomachs weren't evidence enough that there was no such thing as "too many groceries." Neta would remember the first time her mother told Neta she was pretty, insinuating she could sleep her way to money or drugs or a comfortable home with running water.

That image was snapped in Neta's mind's eye years before her grandparents intervened and helped raise her. Years before they paid for one rehab facility after another for their daughter. To Neta, it was her mother's bottom though she knew there were almost certainly trap doors in that floor. Other depths. Worse images.

Neta couldn't remember a single parent-teacher conference her mother attended. Not a church meeting, even though she and Henry would go, sitting in the back so they could pilfer donuts slick with shimmering glaze. Isabell helped Neta with homework while Lottie cooked supper, boiled baked beans loaded with hotdogs and salt and packets of ketchup on good nights. Her mother was a peripheral blur in her childhood while her siblings and, later her grandparents, were the focus.

Now, Neta moved every few months because she could. Because the curio cabinet of haunted memories would seize her, wrapping its bony fingers around her throat until she was choked with longing and regret. Longing for Lottie and Isabell and Henry. Longing for a do-over. Longing for her mother. Regret that she alone escaped their home unscathed. Still, she kept the same house number, one she gave her students at the community college and her siblings. Henry alone called.

After the most recent move, Neta was engrossed in these memories. So engrossed in fact, when the phone rang, she jumped. Her therapist said she had PTSD. Her memories were triggers which lived alongside depression and loneliness. She bashed the power button on the cordless phone and heard a familiar automated voice informing her it was Henry. Then, with a subtle click, her brother's voice—buoyant and energetic—pierced through the line.

"Netty," he said. She thought she could hear his smile. This was her favorite time of the week. "How is my sister?"

Neta popped one finger after another until she got to her thumbs. She stared at the short knobby squares. The same stumpy thumbs as her sisters and her father and Henry. She wondered how they were all still chained together. Then she heard Henry's whistle, low and patient, calling her back.

"I was just reading," Neta lied. "How are you?"

Henry was serving three to five in a minimum-security prison in southern West Virginia. It wasn't his first stint. Neta listened as he taped a rhythm against the black, plastic pay phone. Henry could've been a wonderful musician. He could pick up any instrument and play.

"Let's talk about Mama."

The two of them let the sentence linger. Neta knew they'd been in contact. That her mother regularly wrote Henry and even sent money once, but they hadn't spoken about their mother for months. Henry broke the silence.

"You need to go see her Netty."

She resented Henry for asking her, though, Neta knew she wasn't really allowed to resent Henry for anything. Gratitude rose to her lips but she pushed it down, suffocated under a feather pillow in her comfortable home. She rocked back and forth, hugging her knees and lightly humming to herself, the phone sandwiched between her ear and her shoulder. Henry's side of the line was surprising quiet. Neta glanced around her apartment. In one corner, there was a tall bookshelf with all the books she didn't read as a child. Everything Judy Blume wrote. The Ramona series, Roald Dahl, Nancy Drew, Shel Silverstein. She stood and crossed the room. She ran her hand along the spines. She counted the books, holding the figure in her head. She wondered what it would have been like as a child to crack the spine of a new book, a book she owned, and smell the crisp fresh paper.

"Mama did nothing for us," she said, a sigh pushing against her gut. "Nothing."

"She's our Mom, Netty," Henry said. "She gave birth to us."

Neta wondered if that was positive or negative. Four kids. Who had four kids in the coal fields? Who had four kids when they couldn't afford one? She wondered for the hundredth time. A woman's voice echoed through the line, announcing they had one minute before the call would be disconnected.

Neta thought of Henry in his orange jumpsuit, sitting in a jail cell for breaking and entering this time though he'd done time for selling drugs too. *Just a fuck up like Mama*, he'd claim but she didn't see it that way. Her mother made her decisions. Henry's were a result of circumstances forced upon him.

"It's family day," Henry said. "Have a heart."

Neta listened to her brother's far away voice. Static crackled over the line as he spoke.

"Okay," she said, resigned.

They hadn't talked to Lottie since she'd married a pious and abusive man from Logan. Hadn't seen Isabell since she'd taken up their mother's favorite pastime.

Neta heard a click as the call disconnected. Her breath was ragged and uneven. She took her pulse, counting the rhythm as it banged aggressively inside her chest cavity. She tried to calm herself, reading the first few pages of the book from her box. When that didn't work, she imagined the beach, the one Henry had taken her to as a child.

It was right before his sentencing the first time. Henry was nineteen and she was six. He drove her in a friend's car to the North Carolina shore, the engine making a loud banging sound the entire way like pennies rattled in a jar. Kitty Hawk. She remembered saying the words over and over and over again to herself. Kitty Hawk. Kitty Hawk. Kitty Hawk. She said it in a sweet little whisper as they drove. It was the song repeated again and again. The two words together sounded exactly right and entirely absurd.

Neta hadn't seen anything like sand dunes. They were like snow piles in the mountains, rising and falling in an endless, colorless expanse. But sand was better. Her toes sank into it easily and immediately she felt warm all over as the sun inched its way across her bare skin. The ocean looked as if it went on forever, married to the sky in its vast endlessness.

Henry rolled up his pants when they reached the shore. He took hers off. He was going to allow her to run through the sand in her hand-me down panties but he said they looked so sad, sagging in the bottom with pearl sized holes eaten in the sides. He put Neta's jeans back on and carried her to a surf store at the top of a tall mountain of sand and sea grass. The sign above it was shaped like a surfboard.

"Pick the one you want," Henry said, opening his arms wide. There were rows of stretchy nylon suits in every possible color and pattern. Blue, green, purple. Yellow polka dots. Pink stripes. She ran her hands over the curved hangers, the metal cool beneath her palms. She slid her child-sized fists towards the middle of the row, enjoying the scraping sound metal against metal made as she browsed. She pulled one from the rack. It was red with ruffles down the center, a bundle of roses at the hip. It clipped around the neck. To this day, it's the prettiest swimsuit Neta ever owned.

Henry reached into his pocket, extracting some of the money he'd saved from selling Mama's drugs. He bought her the tiny suit and a disposal camera that sat near the register. He used their bathroom to help her change, peeling the sticky strip from the crotch. Neta looked at herself in the mirror. She was thin, could've probably gotten by with a smaller size but tags and stickers had already been removed. Plus, she was used to clothes being too big.

"When you were a baby, not even two, I told you I would take you to a real beach," Henry said, hugging Neta's lithe body to his own.

As they exited the store, she ran head-long towards the ocean, her toes burning slightly in the sand. She stared at the water, afraid to enter. It was the color of beer bottles. She allowed the waves to lick her toes. Henry plowed forward, splashing her as he went. The water was salty and delicious as it grazed her upper lip. He held his arms wide, so wide he nearly blocked the sun.

"Netty," he cried, and she ran to him. He picked her up, dangling her legs into the water so the spray ricocheted off their arms. Henry rubbed his nose against Neta's. They were the same noses, round buttons that turned up at the end. Freckles speckled across the bridge.

"Netty, this is the beach," he yelled.

He put her down and for a moment, her legs were unsteady. Wobbly and uncertain, as if her appendages realized she couldn't support herself without Henry's arms. Henry sat in the waves and Neta curled into his lap, resting her head in the pillow beneath his chin.

"Neta," he paused. "I have to leave for a little while."

She looked up at him. He was pale, so pale she wondered momentarily if he was a ghost.

"Lottie will take care of you," he said. "Isabell will send money."

She tried hard not to cry. She sang her song, *Kitty Hawk Kitty Hawk Kitty Hawk*, to herself. She didn't want Henry to go. Neta made a fist and threw it into the glove of Henry's hand.

"No," she said. It was the only word she could muster, so she said it again. "No."

Henry picked her hand up. He kissed her knuckles.

"I messed up Netty," he said. "I messed up good this time."

Neta noticed cigarette buds floating in the frothy waves. She stared, watching the water digest them. Pelicans swooped low, skimming the shallow water and emerging with wriggling fish. She watched one bird, hungry and eager. He dove into the glass bottled water again and again, never catching a fish.

Henry continued to talk. To explain. He sat her in the sand, and for the first time, she felt the uneasy itchiness it produced. She shifted uncomfortably, digging her crescent nails into her thighs. Henry kept dipping his head low, angling to look into Neta's eyes. She avoided him. He picked up three black seashells and pressed them into her hands. She was surprised by how happy the tiny treasures made her. He sat behind her, dangling a long arm over her shoulders and snapped a quick picture of the two of them.

Now, Neta stared at the phone. She willed it to ring again. Praying for one more moment to explain herself to her brother. She knew prison didn't work that way. Still, she hoped.

"Kitty Hawk," she said into the air of her empty apartment, wishing she could taste the balmy ocean breeze as it exfoliated her limbs. Wanting to breathe in the freedom that had once permeated her brother's skin, a smell that was now permanently erased.

The entrance to Four Circles Rehabilitation & Care Center was beautiful and upscale with natural stone stairs and a fountain in the circular portico. The visitors' center was a wide log building with a green paneled roof. It reminded Neta of the Lincoln Logs she played with in preschool. Children and adults, all a little wary, waited in a long security line for admittance. She hadn't seen her mother in years. She was uncertain she would recognize her. She fingered the buttons on her cellphone, flipping it opened and closed with a muffled snap.

A small girl in front of Neta ran circles around her father's legs. She was engrossed, captivated by the child's lopsided pigtails. The way her clothes hung in a precarious angle from her, as if her father had dressed her without taking a moment to shift the shoulders of her shirt back. As they neared the entrance, the girl's father carried her through. A tall guard dressed entirely in black waved a wand over the girl's shoulders. Neta followed them, pushing her compact black purse through the x-ray conveyor belt.

The little girl carried a small paper sack. She shook it up and down and Neta heard something softly flicking the side of the paper.

Neta was now very near the girl, following in a slow progressive line that admitted them into the waiting room. She was drawn to her the way people say they are called to look directly at the sun during an eclipse despite warnings. The girl smiled, the action revealing perfectly round, apple cheeks and a missing front tooth.

"I lost my tooth while Mama was at camp," she said, holding up the paper bag. "I'm going to let Mama put the tooth under her pillow. She doesn't believe in magic, but I do."

The child said this in one big breath, a confession of sorts.

She smiled, shirking back a little. The girl was so sweet and talkative. Neta wondered if she had ever been so irreproachable. The father put her down, her Mary Janes making a squeaking sound as she sashayed around the room. Nurses were lined in crisp scrubs in front of a desk. She smoothed her black dress and twisted her grandmother's ring around her pointer finger. The gold dug lightly into her skin.

"Please check in first, get your visitors' badge," the nurses suggested to those waiting. Each of attendants held clipboards with lists attached to them. Neta assumed it was either a list of pre-approved visitors or a compilation of patients participating. She wondered if her name was on a list? If Henry or one of her sisters had attended to that? Or perhaps her mother, in a hopeful moment of delusion, thought her youngest child would come and sit by her bedside? Did she know Neta lived so close, twenty minutes away?

There was a line of chairs against the back wall of the room. They were heavy, wrought iron, with floral patterned cushions. She sat next to the father/daughter duo. She wanted to ask the father, a handsome man with a broad smile and dimples and thick brown hair, whether his wife was addicted to oxy or heroin or coke. Those were the big three in places like this one. The little girl made her think better of her senseless questioning though. She shook the bag again, bringing it close to Neta's face before her father could reign her in, pulling her back against his chest. The girl wore a long-sleeved shirt with a Peter Pan collar and a corduroy skirt with thick, sweater-like tights underneath. She had curled wings around her temples, hair unwilling to be tamed.

The nurses were walking laps around the room, gathering people in the center where they had laid cookies and a punch bowl.

"My mommy has been asking to see me," the little girl said, interrupting Neta's thoughts as her father hushed her.

Neta touched the father's forearm. "She's okay," she reassured him. "My name's Neta," she extended her hand to the child. The little girl punched it, her fist fitting perfectly into Neta's palm. The father shook his head, a resigned *kids will be kids* look on his face.

"I'm Sage," the little girl said. A nurse approached the father and his forehead crinkled with worry. Around them people were being taken into the bowels of the facility, balancing their cookies and miniature cups of punch as they walked.

"Do you mind?" her father asked, turning and placing Sage delicately in the padded chair next to Neta. The father and the nurse stepped to one side.

"Do you want to see my tooth?" Sage asked, her eyebrows wiggling together in a mesmerizing dance. Before Neta had time to process the question, the little girl was unrolling the bag, sliding her tooth from it. She held it in her palm, extending it to Neta for inspection. She took the tooth, rolled it between her thumb and pointer finger. It was a perfect ecru square except for one thin line of curled white enamel, the root. Neta could no longer remember if it hurt or not, having your tooth pulled. From the corner of her eye, she could see the father's hands flailing aggressively. Had anything been near them, he would've knocked it over. Neta couldn't hear what upset him.

"Did it hurt?" she asked Sage, partially as a distraction to the observant child. Partially as a distraction to herself.

"You've lost teeth before," Sage said. "You remember what it feels like."

Neta didn't but she refused to say as much. The father stopped talking to the nurse and sat, his head in his hands, next to Sage. He scratched his neck, unwilling or utterly incapable of making eye contact. The nurse approached, asking Neta's name and her mother's.

"I'm Neta Daines. My mother is Elsie."

The father was talking to Sage but the girl kept pushing him from her, shoving with tiny, resistant, useless fists that weren't made to harm.

"You can follow me," the nurse said.

She stood. Sage was crying loudly now, her adorable face made ugly with pain.

"You promised," she whimpered, her lower lip curled in a pout. "You promised I could see her today. I need to show her my tooth. To give it to Mama."

Neta meant to walk away. She meant to glide down the hallway and do one of the only things her brother had ever asked her to do. One of the hardest things he could've requested. She stopped though, pivoting on her heel and kneeling before Sage.

"I'll take your tooth to your Mom. What's her name?"

"Mama," Sage said slowly, unwilling to recognize that as a title, an honor, rather than a name. *She'll learn*, Neta thought.

"What should I tell her?" Neta asked. She spoke slowly, more slowly than her natural cadence, accentuating each syllable.

"That it's from me ... Sage," the girl said, pointing forcefully to her own chest. "That it's a piece of me." She bit her lip and Neta knew she was trying very hard to stop crying. She locked eyes with the father, trying to pen an agreement. *Please don't bring her back here. Please don't let that woman hurt her anymore.* Neta's eyes bulged and the contacts within them slid to the left.

Sage slithered the tooth from the paper bag, placing it in Neta's hand. She folded Neta's fingers over it, a firm fist protecting the enamel.

"Amelia Wilder," the father said, still unable to make eye contact.

Neta nodded, allowing the nurse to lead her through a pair of sliding doors. She thought of all the things she wished her mother had done. All the things she wished she knew. All the things she wished she fought for. She opened her fist, staring at the perfect square. Remembering what it felt like to be so proud, so hopeful, and then, suddenly, so disappointed. She pinched the root, remembering Sage's words.

*It's a piece of me*, she had said.

How many pieces of herself had she broken off and handed to her mother? How many sacrifices had they made for Mama's habits?

She pictured Isabell's lopsided braids. Lottie standing in the kitchen cooking dinner, never stopping to complain. Henry caged in a jumpsuit and then, his spinning frame free on the beach. The tooth felt small but purposeful in her hand as she walked away.

Her mother's spine was straight and her eyes clear when Neta reached her room. She was perched at the edge of the bed, her hair combed neatly from her face. Neta didn't remember her mother being pretty and yet, there were still glimpses of youth around her eyes. She wondered how the drugs hadn't stolen that. Neta sat in a chair across from her. She still had Sage's tooth clenched in her hand and she wondered momentarily about the oddity of her life. She was sitting in a chair five hours from West Virginia estranged from most of her family, having never known, or at least not really knowing, her mother. Her grandparents who'd saved her were dead. Her sisters who'd saved her were struggling. Her brother who'd saved her would never truly know the ease of freedom. She was sitting in a chair with the woman who'd carried her for nine months, clutching someone else's tooth. Neta remembered reading that teeth were the strongest part of your body and yet, nothing is invincible.

"Neta," her mother said with a sigh. "I'd hoped but never thought it would be you."

Her voice had a strange cadence, a lilt Neta didn't recognize. It was like a mermaid's siren song.

"Elsie," Neta said coldly.

Why couldn't she be a mother? Why couldn't she quit? Why weren't they more important than the contents of a plastic bag?

Her mother started to murmur, ramble really. Ringing her hands. Finally, Neta put her hand up.

"Do you know Amelia Wilder?"

Her mother thought for a long time. She gestured to one of the nurses who came in so they could ask. The nurse was kind but abrupt.

"Pretty girl. Hangs out in the common room a lot. Has striking green eyes."

Neta wanted to ask more but didn't. Instead, she stood and moved closer to her mother. She wanted to touch her but couldn't.

"You're tall Netty. I don't remember that."

*She wouldn't*, Neta thought. Neta took in the sparse contents of the room. There was a bed with soft white sheets and a blue quilt. A matching oak dresser and nightstand. A flimsy flyer for family day alongside a pile of books. Neta pulled *The Giver* from the pile. She opened it and pressed her nose in it.

She hadn't realized her mother was standing behind her, just in her shadow, until she felt a hand on her elbow.

"You did that as a child. When Henry would bring you a book, you'd smell it."

Neta hadn't known the habit existed that long. She hadn't realized her mother had been watching.

"Now, I do it too."

Neta smiled unintentionally. Her mother strode to the other side of the room. She shifted through the t-shirts and sweaters. From the drawer she pulled a swath of red fabric.

"I've carried this with me for a while but, it's yours."

Neta's fist unclenched and she nearly dropped Sage's tooth. She unfurled a tiny swimsuit that clasped around the neck, a frayed bundle of roses on the hip.

"Kitty Hawk," Neta said aloud.

"Henry brought it to me before his first stint. Said it was something to get out of bed for. That you were something to get out of bed for. I'm so sorry I missed you," her mother said.

Neta didn't trust the words but she wanted to. She hugged the tiny swimsuit.

"Mama," she said.

Neta didn't make eye contact for fear the moment would be broken. Instead, she spoke to the floor tiles.

"I need you to do something for me," she said.

Neta dropped Sage's tooth into her mother's palm and they both stared at the pearly bud.

"I need you to tell Amelia Wilder she has something to get out of bed for."

Her mother nodded and Neta wondered if she would come back. If she could have her family. If her mother recognized all the things she couldn't, wouldn't know. Neta used the swimsuit to wipe fresh tears from her eyes. She imagined replacing the plastic baggie with this thing her mother carried. This thing Henry bought. This glaring, magical talisman that had somehow come to represent hope.

# *Fear*

THIS morning, as I dress my daughter and son, I hear a gun shot. It rings out through suburbia, a sound like the zap of a bug being fried on a summer evening. It could be a car back-firing or *Law & Order* droning in the background. Or it could be a gun. It doesn't affect me. I don't stop to investigate, too absorbed in packing lunches. A salami sandwich for him, a square of baked mac and cheese for her.

I dress them in Christmas colors because the holiday is close. My daughter wears an oversized red bow perched in her fuzzy curls. My son's plaid shirt stretches across his slender shoulders. The morning is hectic but no more hectic than other mornings. It's the ebb and flow of normalcy.

I write notes on napkins—one for each baby that says I love them. A lopsided heart on the pliable fabric for each. I fail to kiss them though as I buckle them into their booster seats. My lips are shiny with gloss and I don't want to disturb the smooth creaminess of their cheeks. Still, I stare at the dimple engraved on my son's cheek. The freckle that dots my daughter's ear.

Drop off is a normal deluge of cars with pristine bumper stickers all claiming the drivers raise honor students. All the SUVs black. All the mini vans white. My kids hop from the car. Their backpacks—hers pink and white striped, his embossed with posed Spider-Man—ride up and down their spines. My daughter half-walks, half-skips, playing lightly with the collar of her dress. They hold hands as they walk into school and I think how nice it is that they are only fourteen months apart. That they share the school's tiny hallways. That they still believe in Santa and Elf on the Shelf and the healing power of sugar. I have presents to wrap and gold-foil Christmas cards to send. Stocking stuffers still need to be bought.

Gas curls like a twisted tail behind me as I leave.

The phone rings as I wrap presents. The words "gunman" and "elementary school" sound foreign sandwiched together. I think it's a cruel joke as they collide, side-by-side in my ears. In my mind. I don't rush to the school parking lot to wait though. Too scared of what I will find. I wrap an American girl doll for my daughter, a plastic stegosaurus for my son. I count the gifts, wondering where they will go if my kids don't come home.

The parking lot is a massive ball of tears. Children line up at one end. I scan the crowd, relieved to spot the red and blue checkered plaid of my son's shirt. His face is pale against the bruised sky and I pray for rain. Rain to rinse away the ache in the air. To reset the Earth.

I can't get to my son right away, held behind a yellow line of tape as I scan the crowd for my daughter's frizzy ponytail, the red bow a beacon I can't miss.

All those gifts waiting for her hands. A doll and a set of blocks. A paint set and a miniature pink guitar.

I remember the morning. Little hands braided together. A brown freckle on the tip of her ear that deserved to be kissed.

I start to cry and lift my arms instinctually. They are empty frames to hold my babies. My son sees me and tries to claw through the line. A teacher I don't recognize restrains him. More students pour from the school and shrieks of pain and joy and fear pound the air.

I remember how my daughter did everything early. She sat up, walked, talked before all the other children in her class. Sharp nubs of teeth sliced through her gums while she breastfed.

Why didn't I kiss her? Hug her? Why didn't I tell her I loved her this morning? Children's minds are so fickle and fragile. Did she know?

As more children, none of them her, reach the lot I list the things she loves. Dolls, art, the color pink. Her brother, her father, me, ballet, violin, tap shoes, fancy clothes, lipstick and nail polish. Eloise books. *Bubble Guppies* cartoons. The list is too short.

A police office with a megaphone requests a single file line of parents. I keep my eyes on my son. When I reach the front of the line, a man asks me to remain calm before I realize I'm weeping and ripping at the skin on my chest. I'm begging … Please … Please …. *Please!* It's a prayer of sorts. A mantra. A pledge. A promise to do better, be more. To no longer get caught up in the exhaustion of parenting. To no longer yell. To love her easily without the complexity that parenting always produces. Please! Please … *please!*

More children running, running, running against the crisp grass slick with frost and, as I say the prayer once more, the peripheral blur of a bright red bow careening towards me.

# Short Dogs, Tall Grass

## Rosa O'Neil

THE people who lived on Bolt Mountain had lived there for their entire lives, as had their parents and grandparents before them. It was as if they were raised from the dirt and peaks that surrounded them, mined from the coal beneath them. The ash from burnt coal ran in their veins, coursed through their circulatory system, and pumped their hearts. So they married their high school sweethearts, if they married at all. They waited tables or worked long night shifts in the mines. They took vacations—once every few years— to Myrtle Beach. They stayed in seedy motels they didn't find seedy because there were wide blue swimming pools to float in, which made them forget the scratchy comforters and the bathrooms that reeked of mildew because they were carpeted. They lived in trailers or small single-story houses inches from the road and miles from the wealthier few—doctors and lawyers and dentists— who they called townies.

At night the people on Bolt didn't listen to crickets or the breeze. They heard trucks heavy with black coal nuggets driving too fast, the wind catching beneath their cabs. Sometimes the coal would fly off, zip down between the homes with a ping against trailers. Kids on Bolt collected the errant pieces the way other children collected seashells. They lined trailer windows and small, easy-to-assemble Walmart bookshelves. They were proud—too proud—of where they came from and too wary of money and strangers and liberals to want to be anywhere else.

Rosa O'Neil was one of them, and damn proud of it. She was nineteen when she'd had her only child, Becca, and Becca had continued that tradition, falling in love with a pill-popping kid and having his twins at seventeen. Being a grandmother in your thirties wasn't so remarkable on Bolt, and Rosa eased into the role. She was fine as long as she had Becca. Then one day, she didn't.

Rosa had watched lots of people leave. Her boyfriend, the father of her baby, Mama. People think you get hard, invincible to the pain. But in reality the cuts got stretched, pried further apart. When Becca left, her pockets heavy with pills and her granny's engagement ring to pawn, Rosa felt like someone had cracked her chest open and shot it with a BB gun. The babies were just three months old, pink and shriveled and constantly awake. Becca had seemed happy to have the babies outside her, relieved to feel more like herself. Her self was an addict though.

Rosa had seen long white stains on her dresser. Residue, as they say on "Law and Order." There were other signs too. The way Becca's pretty eyes couldn't focus. An arrest at the old folks home where Becca had tried to steal prescriptions. The pawnshop receipts and that boy. That boy coming around and wanting stuff. Asking Becca for rides. For money. For sex. Right after Becca popped those twins out, that boy was on top of her. Rosa walked in on them mounted like dogs in heat.

As her daughter shoved the contents of her life into a torn canvas backpack, her neck covered in the purple hickeys, Rosa grabbed one of the babies. It was scrawny and wailing. Its face nearly the same color as Becca's love bites. The baby's toes were curled under, and his back arched.

"You're going to miss everything," Rosa said, holding her grandson under the armpits and not supporting his head. Becca laughed at the lame attempt at guilt.

"Happy to miss that caterwauling," she said.

As she headed down the front stoop, Rosa was sure she saw her skip, her heels lifted slightly off the ground. That boy was waiting in a white jeep stained gray from the coal dust. His shirt was torn at the collar, and he had a giant wad of tobacco in the left corner of his cheek. He raised a pill bottle in his left hand, shook it vigorously.

"Hillbilly mating call," he said and spit a big wad of tobacco juice and saliva into Rosa's grass. Becca cackled like it was the funniest damn thing she'd ever heard, her head thrown back and her eyes closed tight.

"Girl, you're a short dog in tall grass," Rosa said, using her dead daddy's favorite expression. "You'll be back." Then closer, in her grandson's face, "She'll be back."

The car tires squealed as they turned onto Bolt and she was gone. A ghost.

Rosa never really forgave Kyle, her grandson, for being unable to convince Becca to stay. Plus Kaylie, her granddaughter, was the smart one. Rosa learned that quick.

When the twins were young, Rosa took them to a public pool. There was a low fence and patches of grass browned from chlorine. The bathrooms were littered with murky puddles. The twins splashed one another as they paddled into the warm water of the shallow end, their plastic water wings peeking from the pool. Kaylie would hold Kyle beneath the water, counting loudly to three before she let him up, sputtering and splashing and gulping for air. When they were hungry, Rosa paid a teenage attendant at the snack bar for ice cream. She watched Kaylie eat her pushup greedily. Her mouth tinged orange. Her tongue aggressively shoved the bright sherbet from the stick. From the corner of her eye, Rosa saw Kaylie pinch her own arm. A red welt rose instantaneously. Kaylie slipped her wet, sticky hand around Rosa's knee, whimpering softly.

"Kyle pinched me and I dropped the ice cream," Kaylie said, her eyes wide and doe-like.

Rosa didn't have cash for another ice cream. She stared down at the little girl. So much like Becca. So different. Kyle sucked ignorantly on his pushup, sticky liquid looping around his thin wrists to form a multi-colored bracelet.

"Share with your sister," Rosa said sternly.

Kyle's eyes stayed on his toes as he handed the sloppy snack to Kaylie without complaint. Rosa didn't bother monitoring how many licks each child got. Didn't count or time or tell Kaylie to hand the ice cream back. Rosa believed in survival of the fittest. Hadn't she learned the difference between a table that tips well and one that won't? Hell, she'd even grabbed tips for other waitresses some nights. So she understood Kaylie's con. She liked it. She rewarded it. Kaylie understood that stepping on someone's back might be your only leg up.

As she grew into a teenager, Kaylie didn't look like Becca, but she was still smart like her, capable. If this girl could survive Bolt, Rosa knew she could be something. Not that Rosa wanted her to leave. Rosa imagined she'd go to school in Morgantown, study to be a nurse, and then she'd come home to take care of her with none of Becca's preclusions for drugs or dirt-bags. Kaylie was Rosa's second chance.

Surprisingly, as she got older, Kaylie's temperament only improved. She would rub Aspercream on Rosa's aching shoulders after long shifts at IHOP. She'd record "General Hospital" and, pressed in a tightknit bundle, the two would watch together. Kyle would fold himself on the floor at their feet, reading or just bothering them with questions.

"Sonny is so handsome," Kaylie said, her head resting on Rosa's shoulder as the smarmy gangster's face filled the television screen. The house smelled of warm pepperoni rolls, like fresh biscuits and olive oil and meat slick with grease. Rosa didn't like Kaylie's taste in men, but she was happy she hadn't brought boys around yet.

Kyle clicked a pen, the sound interrupting the cinematic music of the soap. He stood to retrieve the pepperoni rolls from the oven. While he was gone, the familiar popping sounds, television gunfire, filled the room.

"What happened?" Kyle hollered, stomping through the house, his feet loud despite the shag carpeting. His voice urgent.

"Why do you care?" Kaylie teased, and Kyle blushed crimson. He flopped back onto the floor.

"Rolls are ready," he said, staring at the television screen despite himself.

Kyle was too simple for his own good. He was skinny, his ribs exposed like a skinned fish and his wrists as tiny and fragile as a child, even as he grew. His gestures didn't help garner any of Rosa's sympathy. The way he flipped that red hair out of his eyes with an exaggerated whip, laughing hard and long. It was flamboyant. She decided early and often that he was stupid, a follower. Rosa knew he'd go to jail. Most boys on Bolt did for drugs or petty theft or vandalism, if not something more serious. Rosa remembered Kyle's father jiggling that bottle with relish. *Hillbilly mating call.* She couldn't find any of Becca in Kyle.

When they were all together, clustered close in the living room around the T.V., Rosa couldn't help but think of her favorite movie, *Sophie's Choice*. She'd rented it from Blockbuster when she was pregnant with Becca, her belly and ankles fat and swollen, acne scars and stretch marks covering her skin from the increased hormones. There was something about the story, the way Meryl Streep wept as she begged the Nazis to take both babies, kill them both. She couldn't choose but then chose in the end. Sometimes Rosa lined things up in her mind, asking herself what would fall and what she was willing to save? The Twinkie, the pepperoni roll, the Doritos? "General Hospital," "Dynasty," "Days of Our Lives?" Daddy, Mama, Becca? Then, after the squalling and the fighting and the tears —Kaylie and Kyle. It sometimes surprised her that the answers were the same, even on the bad days, the early days when Kaylie had colic. They were what she saw on an endless loop. The pepperoni roll, "General Hospital," Becca, Kaylie. The survivors were ever-present, a line of decisiveness that circumstances or the day's events couldn't shake. Rosa's favorites were pre-destined and she welcomed the game in all its morbidity.

### Kyle O'Neil

You weren't gay on Bolt Mountain. You were different, or weird. "Closeted" is how Kyle preferred to think about it. He'd known since he was a little boy. He wanted dolls and nail polish. He wanted to watch soap operas with Nana Rosa and Kaylie, and he wanted to dye Nana Rosa's hair for her. He wanted to teach her to be beautiful instead of watching her pluck her eyebrows in thin straight lines. Mostly though, he wanted to tell someone his secret.

The most obvious choice would be his sister but, no matter what Kyle said or did, he couldn't get close to Kaylie. Kyle did both their homework, sitting in front of the couch with algebra books sprawled across his lap. He helped her with boys, sliding notes through the holes in lockers requesting they meet in the smoke hole behind the girls' bathroom. He chauffeured her to school and back, never asking for gas money.

In return, Kaylie spent most of her time ignoring him. She was popular in the way most girls on the mountain were popular, because she put out and could chug a beer. She had a way of slipping her arms around the waist of buff football players as they did a whispered dance down the crowded hallways. The only fight Kyle ever got in was when he heard Johnny Gant call her a butter face in the boy's locker room.

"What's that?" another boy asked as he tied a pair of New Balance sneakers. Before his sister's name was mentioned, Kyle was trying to avoid being noticed.

"You know," Johnny said, explicitly thrusting his pelvis forward. "Everything's hot, *but her* face."

Kyle shoved Johnny into the lockers, using his thin shoulders as a weapon. He knew he'd only get one good hit. He raised a fist, his thumb shamefully folded under his fingers, but he didn't get a chance to throw it. One of the other boys wrenched his arm backwards pinning it behind his back. Johnny got close to Kyle's face.

"Listen," he said, spitting slightly. "I'll say what I want. I'll fuck her when I want."

Kyle hadn't realized how handsome Johnny was until he was that close. He had thick blond hair and blue eyes. He was thin with dimples you could stumble into. Kyle hardly noticed the cauliflower ear from wrestling. Then, as the boys shuffled past Kyle towards the door, he heard Johnny's last word.

"Faggot," he said snickering.

In the months that followed, Kyle tried to forget the word. He was unsure if Johnny knew he was gay or just said the worst thing he could think of to a kid from Bolt. But he observed Johnny making a more concerted effort with Kaylie. He lingered by Kyle's beat-up station wagon, leaning on the passenger door after school. In the cafeteria, Kaylie and Johnny's thighs were glued together, his fingers tip-toeing up and down her spine before resting on her ass. On the way home from school, Kyle tried to tell Kaylie what a jerk Johnny was without saying what he called her.

"He's a jackass," he said, staring hard at the road.

"Why?"

"Kay, he called you a name. A butter face," he said, hoping he wouldn't have to explain the term.

Kaylie laughed hard, her eyes watering at the corners in thin streams.

"At least he thinks my body's good," she said, blowing a big bubble of

Bubble Yum.

Kyle didn't try to explain what Johnny had yelled at him. He was too worried it would open another conversation he wasn't ready for. They didn't speak about Johnny again until skip day.

Every year since eighth grade, Kaylie and Kyle skipped school for an afternoon, riding with friends over the mountain to swim and fish at a fork in the Little Coal River. Nana Rosa didn't mind or didn't know, Kyle couldn't decide which. Sometimes there was fucking but mostly it was music and alcohol. Kyle always drove his station wagon, loaded with beer and swimsuits and Kaylie's friends. Johnny brought wide black inner tubes, and he and Kaylie spent the afternoon sandwiched into one, making out. Kyle drank big gulps of Natty Light, not really enjoying himself. The river smelled like sewage and dead fish carcasses. The beer felt lukewarm and fuzzy as it coated Kyle's throat. Trees surrounded the bend in the river. The roots were fat clumps that ate into the river's edge. Two cardinals sang in the high branches of one maple. Kyle hated how alone he felt.

As everyone was hitching rides home in the back of trucks, Johnny ambled up, the inner tubes deflating beneath his arms. He asked to ride with Kaylie and Kyle. Kaylie and Johnny slid into the backseat while Kyle situated himself behind the low steering wheel, his knees uncomfortably constrained. As he drove, Kyle heard their sloppy kisses. The sound of too much saliva and the smacking of tongues. Kaylie moaned lightly, and Kyle cleared his throat, hoping it was a hint so they would shut the fuck up. Johnny popped the top on two glass bottles of Coors, and between sloppy kisses, they slurped them back. The smell of yeasty beer bubbles filled the car. Kyle took the curves on Bolt hard and fast, grinding Kaylie and Johnny closer together in a fit of laughter.

"Mine's gone," Johnny said.

"Mine too," Kaylie said with a hard laugh, a howl really, that made Kyle glance in the rear view mirror to check on her. He watched her nibble on Johnny's nub of an ear.

"Throw them down," Kyle said. "I'll stop at the Stop 'n Save before we get home."

Before he could really think about what Kaylie was doing, she cranked down the back window. Kaylie had a great arm. She could've pitched for the softball team had she not been so lazy. Kyle remembered watching her aim for the yellow pins at the Coal Festival every summer. Shattering the pyramid of milk bottles as Carnies called, "Knock one down, win a bear." Kyle swerved as he stared into the shallow yard before the trailer park. A little boy, his arms stained with mud and his pants heavy with coal, was building an elaborate pyramid. Kyle glanced into the backseat.

"Don't," he said as Kaylie released the first bottle. Kyle reviewed Johnny's face. His eyes were wide, his mouth dangling open with surprise and excitement. Kaylie launched the other bottle. Both nailed the boy in the forehead. Kyle slowed, began to turn the car around.

"Keep going," Kaylie and Johnny cried in unison, pushing on his shoulders and the back of the seat to urge him forward.

Kyle shoved his foot harder on the gas, leaving skid marks on the asphalt and the child splayed in the grass, unmoving.

Kyle heard the sirens head up the mountain behind his house. Sirens weren't new. They were part of the shit orchestra that serenaded the poor. But part of him knew that the wails were for that little boy who hadn't gotten up. He closed his eyes, opened them again. Kyle kept seeing the boy. He imagined him extending his arms, raising them up to catch the bottles Kaylie threw. They had come down on him with a crash, square in the head. Kyle lay on the couch, popping his fingers and clicking his tongue against the back of his teeth. When Kaylie flopped into the chair beside him, he didn't look over or acknowledge her. She was still wearing the wet swimsuit.

"It's fine," she said, sitting behind his desk. "It's going to be fine."

Kyle thought of all the people he knew in that trailer park. Of all the people they knew on Bolt. There wasn't much chance this would go unnoticed. Kyle leaned onto his forearms and stared at the person he'd shared a womb with.

"Damn Kay, what on Earth?" he spat angrily.

Before she could answer, someone knocked on their front door. Then Kaylie walked calmly from the room, grabbing an old apple from the bowl on the kitchen counter, and turning on her heel, returning to answer the door.

*Lie*, she mouthed.

An officer in a neatly pressed blue uniform stood at their door. He had graduated a few years before Kyle and Kaylie. *Charlie*, Kyle thought, remembering a kid who was beaten with a belt so often, he'd gone to the academy in Beckley to become state police.

"Your nana home?" Charlie asked.

"She's at work. What can we do you for?" Kaylie smiled and gave a wink.

"Who's been driving that station wagon, the Corolla outside?"

Kaylie pivoted, leering at Kyle.

"Company," she said, pointing a thumb towards Charlie. She bit into the side of an apple that had clearly gone bad. The crunch was noticeably absent.

"Officer," Kyle said. He sucked in the sides of his cheeks. "What's going on?"

"Were you kids up at the lake today? Coming home around three-thirty?"

Kyle nodded. "High school tradition." He slouched against the wall, feeling faint.

"Were you drinking?" Charlie looked down at his notepads but didn't move his pencil.

"Yes sir," he said, pulling himself taller. "I had a few."

"You got the empties in the car?" Charlie said. He wasn't aggressive, and for the first time, Kyle considered the fact that he probably hated this job. He probably spent most of his time arresting people he knew.

"No, sir," Kyle said. "We pitched them."

"You hit anything when you threw them?"

Kyle wanted Kaylie to answer but she'd gone into the other room. He thought he heard her whistling lightly. Kyle's instinct was to save himself but then he thought of his twin, the way she refused to ask questions about their mom even though she kept a crumpled picture in her sock drawer. The way she dried the dishes when Nana Rosa washed, their hands in perfect sync as they passed plates back and forth.

"Yeah," he said, turning around so Charlie could more easily slip the cuffs over his wrists. Charlie's grasp was gentle and Kyle realized it was the most any man had touched him.

"Bend your head now," Charlie said, his words wet against Kyle's ear as he pushed him into the backseat of the car.

As Charlie drove Kyle into town, past the Methodist church with its wide white steeple and the IHOP with its blue and red signs and the smell of waffles, Kyle leaned back in the seat and continued to think of the little boy. He wanted to ask if he was dead. Kyle imagined the child was gay too, not because he knew him, but more because Kyle knew there must be another boy on the mountain who felt the way he did. Kyle hoped the boy had been spared some terrible existence on Bolt, like coming out or getting hit or dealing with a drunk daddy. Bolt was full of those. It specialized in bad childhoods.

### Rosa O'Neil

The IHOP was so busy Rosa didn't notice Kaylie at first. She was slumped in a corner by the bathroom with deep worry lines penetrating her forehead. She wore a translucent bikini and no shoes. Kaylie flexed and clutched her fingers, her nerves evident. Rosa wiped the grease from her hands, forcing a stalk of hair behind her ears.

"What's up, kiddo?" Rosa asked, using one arm to draw Kaylie into a hug. She grabbed an apron from a hook inside the kitchen, shoving it harshly into Kaylie's open hands.

"Kyle's in jail," Kaylie said. "County for manslaughter, I think. Or assault. Something. I don't even really know. Charlie Clint arrested him."

Kaylie's words were a long ramble.

"You got some clothes?" Nana Rosa said. She turned in a wide circle, searching for her the canvas bag fat with her dinner and wallet and keys. She hollered back into the kitchen.

"Boys, I got to see about my grandson."

A short man behind a deep fryer gave her a thumbs-up. Rosa briskly rubbed some color back into Kaylie's arms. "He's going to be okay," she said, trying for reassuring. Then low, so low that it was barely audible, she whispered, "What's that damned fool done this time? Ain't a man worth a damn on the whole mountain."

It didn't take long for everyone in town and on the mountain to hear what happened. Charlie told a few people at the grocery. A nurse saw the weeping mother of the injured boy filing a police report. Some customers overheard in the IHOP. Rosa and Kaylie listened as a couple pushed a stroller in front of the police station, discussing the beer bottle boy who might have brain damage. The police station was in the center of town, a squat gray building behind the tall, gold-domed courthouse. Across the street was a brick library and the town's only Mexican restaurant, the sound of mariachi music spilling into the street.

"Today you skipped school," Rosa said. "I can tell as much from what you're wearing. What else do I need to know?"

Kaylie told her about the lake and the ride home. About Johnny Gant.

"I sat up. Kyle wasn't drinking as he drove. I threw two bottles out the window. I wasn't aiming for him, but I hit that little boy."

Rosa saw Kaylie pinch her leg lightly so that fat tears would form. *Alligator tears*, Rosa's daddy had called them. Another con. Rosa momentarily wanted to slap Kaylie, to singe her cheeks. A temporary tattoo of shame. She thought of all the times she'd written Kyle off. All the moments she'd unduly assumed Kyle was the same as his worthless father.

"I don't want to tell them what happened," Kaylie said, her voice hard and distant like an echo. "But I will."

Kaylie scooted over in the seat, rested her head on Rosa's shoulder. She sniffled softly and rubbed Rosa's forearm.

"I didn't mean to," she said again, looking up with a pouty expression Rosa was sure Kaylie thought was endearing. Rosa patted her hand, then kissed her knuckles.

Rosa and Kaylie walked into the jail. At the front desk, they were given visitors badges and led into a room that was gray. A two-way mirror lined the entirety of one wall. A table and four chairs, two on each side, were nailed to the floor.

"You have about ten minutes," a fat officer said to someone Rosa couldn't see. He pushed Kyle into the room. Rosa smoothed her greasy uniform. Tugged lightly on her ear. When Kyle noticed Kaylie's feet were bare he removed his flip-flops, shoving them under the table towards her. Kaylie took them without thanking him.

"You've gotten yourself in a mess," Rosa said, sitting painfully before him. Kaylie leaned against the mirror.

"Don't know if I was alone in that," Kyle said. He wouldn't look at his sister. He scratched his hands, wiped the sweat from behind his neck. "I can't be in here."

Rosa saw the desperation in his face. The fear of being different in this place where everyone needed to fit in.

"Honey, I don't have the scratch to get you out."

Rosa looked across the table at the boy. The two lined themselves up in her mind. Kaylie and Kyle. *You may keep one of your children. The other must go away.* Rosa started towards the door where Kaylie stood.

"Guard," she called. "This girl needs to make her statement." Rosa tried hard to memorize the exact oval of Kaylie's face, the way the sun made natural highlights in her hair.

# Love, Mom

*for Ella and Addie*

TO my girl, my bunny, my sweet sailor mouth Cracker Jack, my Pooh Bear, my love, the bane of my existence and the entirety of my heart—

Your tummy, the one I filled with burnt toast and ginger ale and teaspoons of honey when you were sick, is now solid and round. As I sit here, you've gone into labor. You're in a room with your husband and two nurses and one doctor whose face is covered with a green mask even when he comes out to talk to me in the waiting room. My area, as I think of it now, has a long vinyl sofa and television sets that are too loud. Down the hall, there's a vending machine that hums noisily and I eat Kit-Kat after Kit-Kat, enjoying the smooth chocolate and the noisy crunch, while I wait for your daughter to be born.

A nurse has wheeled you in a chair that squeaks slightly down the white hall. Your hair piled in a high ponytail, the way you wore it when you cheered for high school football games. A brown line stretches from your breastbone to the abyss beneath your stomach. You've complained so much about it, and I couldn't remember, couldn't recollect, if I had been stained in the same place. So I googled it. It's called a Linea Nigra but the name means nothing to me. It still doesn't haul back the memories.

You have griped about all this for weeks. I sat helplessly, unable to make you less pregnant. Unable to take away the pain that rips down your spine, even though I want to believe I have protected you from hardship. To busy myself, I thought I would tell you some secrets of this exclusive club you're joining, the one where you give your time and energy and sleep and, yes, even your body for moments so simple. You won't believe you'll trade all that for a giggle—a toothy exhale that's brief, but shows four blocky white teeth floating in a pink ocean. Or a kiss, which is really all slime on the apple of your cheek. Sacrifice will become part religion, part mantra. My sweetheart, these are the secrets no one will share. Motherhood is a lot like staring directly into the sun, it's blindingly beautiful. The pain and pleasure so intertwined that you can't distinguish one from the other.

*You won't bond immediately and yet, that's the closest you'll ever be to your child.* In the beginning, as you heal from the stitches and your body tries to correct itself, bonding is hard. You were a good sleeper. You fit into my willing arms like a cog in a clock. But when I looked at your long blond lashes and the murky eyes trying to focus, I didn't know you. I didn't know how to stop your crying or how to feed you or when you were supposed to sleep. Nana offered help and I wanted to refuse her but couldn't. She ran the vacuum and made bottles in advance and took you for walks in a stroller down our tree-lined street. She found your preschool that first week, signaled by the pink and orange handprints plastered to the glass. She chatted with babysitters at the park about referrals. But as the pink sky faded to navy, I was alone with you. I sang "Dream a Little Dream of Me" in my tone-deaf alto too loudly. You preferred the record. I made your food too hot. Steam rose from the surface of your bath water.

On your first birthday, I bought yellow balloons and streamers. I dressed you in a white dress with frills at the hem and tied your thin, blond hair in a satin bow. Your daddy blew up an inflatable pool, and we had water balloons even though you couldn't throw them, even though you could've choked on the plastic carcasses left behind. The Big Bird cake I baked looked wobbly and deformed with misshaped white eyes. His feathers more closely resembled fur, and his beak drooped before eventually falling. Big Bird as a stroke victim. I made your aunt climb into a costume. It was a hundred degrees outside and she scared the children, sent loud piercing screams over our freshly mowed lawn and provoked tears when she tore the head off to wipe her sweaty brow. When she changed, we soaked her down with water balloons, and Daddy gave her a beer with icy particles slipping down the side. I wanted the party to be perfect, to highlight what a good mother I was. I wanted it to show that I knew you. But the truth was, my entire life has been a bizarre game of catch up.

*Applying sunscreen to tiny, wriggling bodies is a form of parenting purgatory.* And there are others. Practicing *Twinkle, Twinkle* on the violin with you for a year to hear you squeak through it at a too-long concert in a too-hot church. Teaching you to use a fork, tie your shoes, drive. Watching you leave for college. Let me be clear. Many lives are worse than a normal one. Many are hellish.

Once, when you were barely a year old, you had a seizure. I went to collect you from your nap, and your fingers were clenched claws against the pink muslin sheet. Your eyes were wide globes bulging slightly. You could barely breath, so a purple circle highlighted your mouth. I was sure you would be brain-dead or you would die in my arms. Twenty minutes. I waited twenty minutes for EMTs. They told me to count your breaths. I counted the shallow inhales (86), the number of days you'd been alive (310), the number of words you could say (8), the number of years I'd lived without you (32), the years I could survive if I outlived you (0).

The EMT was handsome. He had deep-set blue eyes and a black beard and a full head of sculpted black hair but I hated him. He kept telling me fibril seizures were "normal." He repeated the word six more times on the two-mile drive.

That was hell, but motherhood is purgatory. It's the everyday nonsense. It's the bath that ends in a watered-down bathroom and wet jeans and moldy rubber ducks. It's the dinners that devolve into schoolyard arguments over green beans until negotiations end with three bites and a smattering of beans littering the kitchen floor. And it's applying sunscreen once every two hours even though you claim you don't need it. Even though you wear a sun shirt. Even though your skin is a deep olive hue like your aunt's.

*Your life will be haunted.* I took twelve weeks off after you were born. I breastfed even though my nipples cracked and I smelled like a three-day old milkshake. I worked and enrolled you in Montessori. I hired tutors when I couldn't teach you myself. I bought corsages when your prom date forgot—pale pink and white roses to match your taffeta gown. I introduced you to powerful women. Sandra Day O'Connor. Liz Taylor. Wonder Woman.

Still, some other life haunts me. The possibility of things I could've done better. The possibility of how I could have been better.

I think of your five fat fingers intertwined with the babysitter's. How you cried for her when she left each evening. How your hugs when I went to work were light, not lingering. How relieved I was after I fired her, even when she cried. Even as your tears made salty semicircles on my t-shirt. You asked for her the next week when we went to the circus and on a picnic a few weeks later. A flimsy kite parallel with the ground that kept getting slapped from the sky reminded you of her kite-flying prowess. Each time you asked, I shrunk. I was microscopic in the realm of your adoration. I told you she was with a new family, a new little girl. The babysitter Facebooked me recently. She has a teenage son with piles of black hair and the beginnings of a moustache. As I accepted her request, I wondered if she would do the same thing in my situation. I wondered if the request was a signal that she'd forgiven me. I wondered if I would be able to forgive myself.

*I hope motherhood shapes but doesn't define you.* Before you were born, your father was lazy but charismatic. My mother called him The Car Salesman as he peacocked around the hospital carrying you like a loaf of bread. After we brought you home, he took a new job. Then, your father became determined and charismatic. He traveled weeks at a time. I pictured him eating in extravagant restaurants with candles lighting his tanned skin, lobsters or porterhouse steaks steaming in front of him. I cast a perception. I was the martyr. Alone with you trying to force-feed mashed carrots and whole milk and scarfing down a hotdog while he was sipping martinis. To this day, I've never actually seen him order a martini.

I envied his ability to cruise into work for eight hours without thinking about the logistics of your life. I found the camps and the sitters, and I was the room parent. I packed healthy lunches and read *I'll Love You Forever*. I sat beside you and taught you to write. I proofread college applications. Yet when the door swung open at the end of the day, you ran headlong into his arms. He twirled you through our house, pecking your cheeks like a barnyard chicken. He let you dance on his black dress shoes. He scooped you from the grass after soccer games when the coach's yelling bruised your ego.

The truth was, he loved you too much. Or rather, too much more than he loved me. On the day I married him, he wore a gray suit that fit him perfectly, like the candy shell that coats M&Ms. His shoes glistened in the afternoon sun. He looked like Cary Grant, and as I slipped down the aisle, his eyes skimmed my body taking in every inch of my petite frame.

When you came, he stopped seeing me as that girl. He saw me in stained t-shirts and ratty pajama bottoms. I wanted someone who would roll up the cuffs of his shirt and change diapers, fix a tire, rock you at two o'clock. Your father wanted someone who would sip champagne at the company Christmas party and buy concert tickets for a Tuesday night.

There's a natural evolution within people. In the course of my life I was a wife and a mother. A librarian. A room mom. A lover. An argument. I was angry and lost and, within you, happy and found. I was useful and useless. My darling, I have learned a lot and I know nothing. Your father was my only other great love. I was a shitty wife. He was a terrible husband. Still, I regret telling him to leave, angry and pointing with a throat sore from yelling. My only other real regret was allowing myself to be two-dimensional, a cardboard cutout of a mother.

*Loneliness isn't synonymous with being alone.* Deep into my pregnancy, I saw a news story about a blue whale that sang so high other whales couldn't hear her.

The image on our black and white screen showed a long, graceful mammal cutting through the water with her massive tail. I fingered my belly button, which had recently popped out while I listened to a reporter call the whale the "matriarch of loneliness." You swam into my hand, brushed my palm as I silently sobbed, blowing my nose on the thin white shirt I wore.

I carried you for forty-two weeks. You were with me as I rode subways stuffed with people exuding pungent body odor. My womb cradled you as I discussed books and wait lists and author readings in a chilly library where I continually wore a shawl. I slept on my side because my belly was so large while your father interrupted sleep with snores so fierce they rattled the mattress. Once you were born, I secured you in a tight wrap and carried you against my chest. Sometimes you slept there, your blond wisps matted with sweat and your cheeks the color of raspberry macaroons.

I was always with you, but loneliness seeped from my pores. I thought people could smell it on me like booze on a frat boy. I kept a journal during that time, a bound leather book where I wrote my feelings each day alongside your schedule. The first entry read, "I cry because I feel lost despite my newfound purpose. Baby slept: 9:30-11; 12-12:15; 3-4:30." Another read, "Wanting to leave is eclipsed by her smile. I wonder if that will always be the case." The entries became shorter and further apart because writing about desolation felt like a recording of my everyday state. I was the blue whale, constantly looking for a matching song but never quite able to locate anyone else.

Your child won't make you whole.

Your husband just came to the window outside my room. He held up your daughter, her hair twisted like a cinnamon bun at the crown. Engraved divots in the chubby flesh where her knuckles will soon be. She cried a high-pitch, gaping wail revealing pink tonsils. She opened her eyes, her mouth forming a wide 'O' as I looked at her. I cried, tears tattooing my cheeks and jawbone, because she is perfect. Because perfect should be enough.

Your daughter is innocent to all this, and I momentarily want to crumple this note and shove it further into the shadows, into the category of the things we shouldn't say.

But one day, we will all shift forward. I will be gone and you will sit in my chair and your beautiful girl will be in a room you aren't allowed in. You'll want to pass along the things you know but that knowledge will feel expired. Irrelevant. The curdled milk of advice and, you'll write it anyway. You'll write because love and money and parents who stay together won't save your daughter from any of this. Because as women, as mothers, we're constantly waiting for the world to change. We're consistently searching for acceptance and love and purpose. And mostly, you'll compose a letter because you long for her life to eclipse your own.

Love, Mom

# Acknowledgements

HUGE thanks go to the entire MFA staff of Converse College in Spartanburg, SC — particularly to my mentors Bob Olmstead, Cary Holladay, Leslie Pietrzyk, and Marlin Barton. Rick Mulkey was instrumental in my acceptance and success throughout the program. Gwen Holt, Angela Raper, Kay Stewart, and Linda Meredith — you are my sanity. Thanks for always listening. Jonathan Burgess, Aaron Jenkins, Russell Jackson, Mackinley Greenlaw, Dr. Russ Carr, and Gabby Freeman also offered support and guidance throughout the writing process and were quick to share my work. Thank you to Rhonda Browning White for introducing me to the Appalachian writing scene. All of you are model literary citizens who are often armed with bourbon.

To the literary magazines and editors who've published my work — most notably Emma at Owl Hollow Press and Rachel at The Same — thank you for the support and guidance. To the journalism department at West Virginia University, particularly the late George Esper, I never would've pursued a career in writing if it wasn't for you. Thanks for never diminishing that spark!

Blair (and Emily), Chas (and Katie), Julie, and Will Armistead are early readers and forever friends. I couldn't survive life without you. Samantha and Linda Crafton became my Chicago family and we formed a book club of sorts. Your words of support and wisdom kept me warm many winter nights. To my extended family, most notably Debbie Sherman and Katrina Newberry, thanks for always reading and supporting me.

Angela Mason was my first friend and, even though she has a rule that she won't read anything sad, she proofed much of my work. Thank goodness someone with insight made you my sister. Josh Mason, with his quick wit, makes vacations more fun. Thanks for being Angela's other half. To my mom and dad – thank you for all the sacrifices I didn't realize you made until I had my own kids. For all the science projects, tennis matches, and sight words you helped me memorize – thank you! Parenting is hard but you always made it look easy.

To my lovely husband Ben – you are always kind. Thank you for giving me the time to write. Last – but certainly not least – to my girls, Ella and Addie (and my surrogate sweeties – Olivia, Henry, and Grace). I write about you, because of you, for you. Thanks for the inspiration!

Some versions of these stories were published or are forthcoming in *Short Story America Volume VI* ("The Fairy House"), *Crack the Spine 2020* ("Fear"), *Donut Factory* ("The Easiest Thing"), *Bluestem Magazine* ("They Always Wave Goodbye") and *Literary Mama* ("Love, Mom"). Thanks to the editors for seeing something within them.

**K**atie Sherman is a journalist and an award-winning author who covers fine food and parenting—two things rarely related—in Charlotte, NC. She has been nominated a number of times for the Pushcart Prize and Best of the Net. Her stories have been short-listed for contests through New Letters, The Same, Short Story America, and Yes Yes Books. She has an MFA in fiction from Converse College, a BA in Journalism from West Virginia University, and an affinity for Southern Gothic literature, cider beer, Chicago, and morning snuggles with her two daughters. Katie has published extensively in literary magazines across the country. This is her debut collection.

CPSIA information can be obtained
at www.ICGtesting.com
Printed in the USA
BVHW041834301021
620339BV00004B/11

9 781646 626311